Long Way Down

Collin Wilcox

Terri Logue

Random House: New York

This book is dedicated to
Jean Muir,
in partial payment of a
big creative debt

One

"Do you want to flip for it?" I pointed to the lunch check.

Friedman shook his head. "I couldn't afford to lose. My wife, the family treasurer, has me on a budget. For the first time since I've been married—twenty years, for God's sake—I'm on a budget."

"Then we'd better have thirds on the coffee. There's no charge."

He snorted ruefully, at the same time signaling for the waitress.

"What's the reason for the budget?" I asked.

"The reason," he answered, "is that my number one son has suddenly decided that he's no longer interested in retreating to the hills and building a sod hut and raising organic food. Instead, he's going to be a big-time agronomist. So he wants to go to college. This is February third. College begins September seventeenth. The tab, I figure, is almost six grand a year, everything in. So I'm on a budget."

"Can't he work?"

Again he snorted. "Last summer, when it looked like he was going to turn hippie for sure, we promised him that if he went to college, he wouldn't have to work his way through. Or, more like it, Clara promised. I just went along."

"I'll bet."

We watched the waitress pour our coffee. Friedman's large, swarthy face was sunk deep into his jowl-mashed collar. His eyes were pensive, his full lips thoughtfully pursed.

1

"You know," he said, "I'm just now—at age forty-six—finally beginning to figure out what it really means to be a Jew. Like, it's a Jewish thing that the oldest son's got to have the best. He's got to amount to something. So to Clara, there's no question about Bernie going to college if he wants to go. No question at all. Literally, she'd wash floors, if that's what it took. And she wouldn't think she was making a sacrifice, either. It's just something that you do, that's all. It's expected. It's a—a cultural reflex." He was staring down into his coffee, blinking pensively. For the first time since I'd known him, Friedman seemed unaccountably diffident, telling me what it meant to be Jewish. Normally, Friedman coasted easily above most men's frailties. On the job, I'd often seen him make life-or-death decisions without the slightest hesitation. If something went wrong—if someone died—he didn't flinch from the decision's responsibility. Friedman always managed to seem imperturbably right, even if he wasn't. Yet now, talking about his family and his religion, he seemed strangely vulnerable.

I didn't want to probe too deeply, but neither did I want to slight his confidence by changing the subject completely. I decided on a compromise. "Were you the oldest son?" I asked.

He sipped the coffee, grimaced at the taste, and put the cup down. "No, I was number two. My older brother, Leonard, went to dental school. He now makes about seventy-five grand a year. In Beverly Hills, naturally."

"So you got aced out of college."

"Well—" He hesitated, then looked up, measuring me with a shrewd sidelong glance. His deceptively soft brown eyes were once more inscrutable: seeing everything, revealing nothing. His voice settled into its accustomed accents—lightly bantering, ironic, dry. "Well, the fact is that I went to a seminary for a couple of years."

"You mean you . . ." In spite of myself, I realized that my mouth was hanging slightly open.

"That's right, poopsie. I was meant to be a rabbi. By your stupefied expression, I can see that I never told you."

"But what—I mean"—I shook my head, frowning as I lamely framed the question—"what happened, anyhow?"

"What happened," he answered, "was that I got stage-struck. Which is something I *know* I never told you. I got hooked on amateur theatricals while I was in the seminary, and my studies suffered—considerably."

"I'll be damned." I gulped down the last of the coffee, staring at him over the cup rim.

"I guess," he continued on the same wry, breezy note, "that I must be in a confiding mood. It's probably the shock of that six-grand bite for college. My life is passing in front of me. And after all, we're co-lieutenants. So if I've got to confide in someone, it might as well be someone of equal rank. I can't very well bare my—"

"What happened when you got stage-struck?"

"I dropped out of the seminary and went to Hollywood, of course. In those days, however, I was slim and suave and eager. Or, anyhow, I *thought* I was suave. But my agent touted me as a character type, which I suppose I was, since agents are always right. Anyhow, I probably had as much talent as the next guy. But talent isn't nearly as important as the pure and simple thick-skinned tenacity it takes to keep your eight-by-ten glossy in circulation long enough for some jerk in a casting office to remember your face when a part comes up. Which is to say years."

"Were you in any movies?"

"As an extra, sure. And I had five words in a Gary Cooper Western. Six words, if you count articles. 'Look out!' I shouted. 'He's got a gun.' Whereupon I dived behind the bar—and into show-biz oblivion."

"You quit?"

"I faced facts. It was in the early fifties, and Hollywood was suffering through one of its numerous recessions. I spent two years floundering around in that recession, plus the year and a half I spent getting my six-word speaking part. Most of the time I was a short-order cook. So finally one day I just gave up. I just said screw it, and I came to San Francisco and got a job—as a short-order cook, naturally. But I knew what I wanted, after three and a half years of those Hollywood unemployment lines."

"What did you want?"

"I wanted the dullsville security of Civil Service," he answered promptly. "I didn't ever want to apply for another job. So when the police exam came up, I took it, even though I never actually could see myself putting the arm on anyone. But I passed the exam, by God. Brilliantly. So it came down to a choice of either cooking some more, or becoming a cop—or maybe a life-insurance salesman, or something. So I became a cop. Whereupon I got married and started to put on weight. My agent, it turned out, was right: I was a character type. Which for a homicide cop is the only type to be." He glanced at his watch, grunted, then signaled the waitress. "I've got to get back. The governor's going to speak in less than an hour."

"What's that got to do with you?"

"Didn't I tell you? No. I've been put in charge of his security. For today, you are in sole charge of the homicide squad. You and the captain, that is."

"Is the governor in town?"

"Of course he's in town, you noodlehead. He's speaking at the Civic Center on welfare reform. That's his newest gimmick, you know: welfare malingerers. The campus radicals have served their purpose, headline-wise. And coming down on the hippies isn't a very good political move, because almost everyone has a hippie or two at home, as who should know better than me. So now his eminence is bearing down on welfare chiselers."

"I hope you enjoy the speech." I counted out my share of the check.

"Christ, I'm not going to the Civic Center, if that's what you mean. I can't stand all that political mumbo jumbo."

"I thought you were in charge of his security."

"This is the age of electronics, Lieutenant. For the entire day,

4

I've got Tach Seven, clear channel. Nothing is too good for the governor."

"So you'll be in the office all day." I smiled as I got to my feet. Friedman's fondness for settling his impressive bulk into his over-size swivel chair was well known. As the junior homicide lieu-tenant, with less than a year on the job, I normally went out into the field while Friedman stayed in the office, calling the shots, hassling with the reporters, and placating the brass. It was an ar-rangement that suited both of us.

As we approached the checkstand, the cashier beckoned to me, holding up a telephone. I gave the check and my share of the money to Friedman, then took the call.

"This is Culligan, Lieutenant. I didn't get you up from the lunch table, did I?"

"No, we're just finishing. What can I do for you?"

"Well, I've got an unidentified Caucasian male. Looks like he's about forty or forty-five. He was well dressed. He was killed last night, probably—knifed. The location is a real run-down apart-ment, one of those storefront jobs. I've been here about an hour. Sigler is here, too, and the lab crew and the M.E. Everything is under control, but I thought I should check with you before they move the body. I mean—" He hesitated. "I mean, the victim's well dressed, like I said. He didn't live here, and he doesn't look like he belongs here. So I thought I'd call you."

"What's the address?"

"436 Hoffman. Right near Elizabeth."

"All right. I'll get Canelli, and we'll be there in twenty minutes. Do you need anything?"

"No, sir. Everything's under control, like I said."

"Good. I'll see you in twenty minutes."

Two

I snapped my safety belt, turned on the radio and nodded for Canelli to get under way. Typically, he narrowly avoided our first potential hazard: a huge reinforced concrete pillar that helped support the Hall of Justice. Canelli had been driving for me about three months. My purpose in choosing him was to shape him up, if possible. Canelli's work habits resembled his driving habits. He seemed to skirt disaster constantly, yet never actually collided with anything. Friedman had been right when he'd observed that Canelli was an Italian schlemiel. Canelli would never shape up. He'd never look like a cop or act like a cop or think like a cop. He would always be a slob, Friedman contended—always a bumbler. Still, a cop who doesn't look like a cop can be a valuable tool, properly used. And Canelli was content to be used. He was both amiable and willing. He was also lucky—incredibly, invariably lucky. Maybe his luck derived from his improbable appearance. He weighed two hundred and forty pounds, shambled when he walked and blinked when he was puzzled. He perspired profusely and frequently sucked at his teeth while he searched for a word. His suit was always wrinkled and he never crushed his hat the same way twice. His face was round and swarthy, like Friedman's. And his eyes, in fact, also resembled Friedman's: soft, brown, and guileless. Yet there the similarity ended. Friedman's innocence was carefully contrived: a deceptively wide-eyed mask that had served him well for many years. Canelli's innocence was genuine. He was the only cop I'd ever known who could get his feelings hurt.

"Where to, Lieutenant?" Canelli asked, slowing for the first traffic light.

"Hoffman near Elizabeth. Go out Howard to Twenty-fourth, and turn right."

"Yessir." We were under way again.

"You'd better get in the right lane," I said. "You have to go right at the next corner, or you'll end up on the freeway."

"Oh. Yeah." He glanced over his shoulder, at the same time turning. An orange Datsun protested.

"Those damn foreign cars are so small you can't see them," Canelli muttered.

I didn't reply.

"That's a Datsun," Canelli offered, studying his late antagonist in the mirror. "My brother has one, and he likes it real well. Of course, he's only got five thousand miles on it."

"What kind of car have you got, Canelli?"

"Oh, I've got an old Ford station wagon. It's about ready to fall apart, but I'm going to drive it till it drops."

"That's the cheapest way."

"I know it. See, Gracie and I, we're saving up, you know. To get married. So that's why I—"

"Inspectors Eleven." I recognized Rayburn's voice, in Communications. I picked up the mike and acknowledged the call.

"We have a 307, Lieutenant Hastings. Repeat: a 307. Can I have your position, please?"

307—Homicide in Progress.

I heard Canelli's low whistle as I spoke into the mike: "We're at Fourteenth Street, proceeding west on Howard."

"Will you please hold your position, sir, and switch your radio to Tach Seven?"

As I changed channels, I frowned. Friedman, I remembered, had said that he . . .

"Frank?" It was Friedman's voice, static-blurred.

As I acknowledged the call, I motioned for Canelli to pull to the curb.

"Just a second, Frank." The radio crackled silently for a moment. Then Friedman's voice came back, all business: "There's a shooting in progress at the Civic Center. The governor's been hit. Can you take charge?"

"Roger. On our way." I urgently motioned to Canelli, who was grinding the starter. Lately, the car had been flooding. I'd been meaning to have it checked. Canelli was sweating, muttering at the dashboard.

"Handle code three," Friedman was saying. "I'll advise Inspector Culligan of your situation. Remain on Tach Seven."

"Roger. Which side of Civic Center?" As I asked the question, our engine caught laboriously. We were lurching away from the curb. I leaned forward to clip the red light to the dashboard and flick the siren switch.

"The east side—the plaza that goes from the library to the city hall."

"We're on our way." I braced myself for the first corner, coming up fast. Canelli's hands, I saw, were white-knuckled on the wheel. He was frowning intently, concentrating on the road. "Are there units on the scene?" I asked. It was an automatic question. If you were going to be the first unit on the scene of a 307, you wanted to know before you got there.

"Affirmative." And as if on cue, reports from the scene began to come over the air, advising Friedman of the situation. Since it was an open channel, reserved for Friedman, the terse voices were jumbled together, like air-to-air chatter during a dogfight.

As I turned up the radio against the siren's wail, I heard: "The ambulances are arriving now, Lieutenant. Three of them. Is that enough?"

"No," Friedman answered. "You'll need at least four. Maybe five. They'll be coming."

"Roger. We're—"

"Spread out," a high-pitched voice cut in. "It didn't come from the crowd, for God's sake."

"It *did* come from the crowd. From the side closest to the library."

"No, it came from the library itself."

"We need more crowd control here. The stewards can't get through. We've got to have—"

"Get sharpshooters. He could start shooting again. He—"

"Let's get tear gas ready. We'll need it any minute, here, if he's in the library."

"What about the customers—the people inside?"

A slow, calm voice said, "I've got what looks like a cardiac case, an elderly woman. Right at the corner of Larkin and McAllister."

I braced myself as we careened into Van Ness. An ambulance was just ahead of us. Farther along, two motorcycle patrolmen were weaving rhythmically through the heavy traffic. I pointed up ahead. "Fall in behind that ambulance, Canelli."

"Right. We'll be there in a half-minute."

"Go up Polk Street—up and around, and down Larkin. Get as close to the library as possible."

"Yessir."

On the radio I could hear Friedman saying, "Lieutenant Hastings is arriving on the scene any minute now. He'll take over. Repeat, Lieutenant Hastings, from Homicide, will take over."

I clicked the mike to "transmit," at the same time pinning my badge to my topcoat. I tossed my hat into the back seat as I said, "This is Lieutenant Hastings. We'll be arriving on Larkin Street, proceeding south. I want a way cleared. I want to get as close to the scene as possible. My car is a green Plymouth sedan. Repeat, a green Plymouth." I grabbed for my sectional scan map. "Any traffic units responding, let's seal off the area bounded by Polk and Hyde, McAllister and Grove Street." More slowly, I repeated the coordinates. As I did, we turned the last corner into Larkin. The traffic was massed solid. We were a block and a half from the scene.

"Park," I said to Canelli. "We'll have to walk."

"Shall I take the shotgun?"

"No, just the walkie-talkie." And into the radio I said, "We have the scene in view, and are proceeding down Larkin on foot. I want all traffic stopped cold in that two-block area. Nobody in, nobody out, except for official vehicles. Nobody moves. I'll be on the scene in one minute. Clear."

I flipped off the radio and got out of the car, carefully locking the door and checking the windows. As I walked, with Canelli puffing beside me, I unbuttoned my topcoat and jacket, then loosened my revolver in its spring holster. Canelli was doing the same.

"Jesus," Canelli breathed. "This is a real mess. I wonder if the governor's dead?"

Three

"I want you to stay right with me," I said to Canelli. "You handle the walkie-talkie net. Let's use channel two."

"Yessir. Right." Half trotting beside me as we crossed Golden Gate Avenue against the light, he switched on his walkie-talkie, awkwardly turning the channel selector and extending the antenna as he walked.

The next intersection was Larkin and McAllister. A half block remained. The dirty gray granite of the state office building blocked our view of the plaza. The sidewalk was crowded with excited citizens, bustling to the scene of violence, their eyes bright, their mouths pursed, their heads straining eagerly forward. The rubber-neckers. God, how I hated them.

A black-and-white car, doors open, radio turned up, was parked so as to partially block McAllister, following my instructions. The library loomed on our left. To our right was the plaza; a dozen steps and we'd have the plaza in sight.

As I shouldered my way rudely through the last scurrying knot of thrill-seekers, I pointed to the black-and-white squad car. "We'll use that one. That's the C.P. I want you to check with Friedman. Then get everyone here tuned to channel two—*fast.*"

"Yessir."

As I reached the McAllister Street sidewalk, I got my first

full view of the Civic Center plaza. A temporary speaker's platform stood at the plaza's center. Hundreds—thousands—were milling around the platform, moving with the characteristic surge of a mob: wild and wanton, yet churning with an ominous, implacable purpose. I could clearly hear the unmistakably low-pitched chittering of the rabble, muttering as it pressed against the platform, seemingly intent on toppling it in their midst, then crushing the survivors. Perhaps twenty persons were packed on the platform, four of them uniformed men. One officer gripped the speaker's microphone. He was slanting the chrome shaft toward him, striking a pop vocalist's foot-braced stance as he harangued the mob, fruitlessly ordering them to make way for the ambulance crews. His voice shook with urgency and anger. I caught a glimpse of two victims, both lying motionless on the platform, both bleeding heavily. One was a woman, the other a man.

Canelli slid into the passenger's seat of the black-and-white, reaching for the mike. The nearest officers were two uniformed men bending over someone stretched out on the sidewalk—the cardiac case, probably. One of the patrolmen carried a walkie-talkie.

Four steps, and I was gripping his shoulder. "What channel are you on?"

Glancing at my badge, he straightened, half saluting. "Channel four, sir." He was a young man with blond hair and a thick reddish mustache.

"Get on channel two. Pass the word: channel two. Is that your car?"

"Yessir."

"I need it."

"Yessir." He turned away, holding his walkie-talkie high in the air with one hand, using the other hand to signal a V for the channel.

"Are there any sergeants here?" I called to the blond patrolman.

"There's one over there." He pointed. "Sergeant Hanley. He's

12

trying to clear a way through the crowd for the ambulance stewards."

"Get him over here. And keep working on channel two."

"Yessir." He was already trotting off, flashing the incongruous V-for-peace sign. Out of the car now, Canelli was doing the same. I put one foot on the squad car's bumper, another on the hood. I stepped up onto the roof of the car.

To my left, a half-dozen patrolmen stood in a haphazard line on the broad steps of the Corinthian-style library. Two of them carried shotguns, one a rifle. Two had walkie-talkies. I could sense their irresolution. A few men had probably gone inside the library. The rest were awaiting developments while they prevented anyone from leaving the building.

To my right, four ambulances were pulled up on the plaza, bordering the edges of the crowd. Another ambulance was arriving, its siren winding down to a guttural mutter. A wedge of officers flailed at the fringe of the crowd closest to me, slowly opening a corridor for the stretchers. One patrolman circled the mob on his motorcycle, urgently motioning the stewards toward the corridor. They were making progress. I glanced at the four streets bordering the plaza. Traffic was stopped, as I had ordered. The casualties would soon be cleared.

It was time to go to work.

I looked down into the seamed, ruddy face of Sergeant Dwight Hanley. I'd known him for nine years, ever since I'd joined the force. Glancing at the circle of upturned civilian faces clustered around my car, I slid off the car's roof to the ground, drawing Hanley aside. "Hello, Dwight. What the hell's happening? Is the governor dead?"

"I don't know. I couldn't get through the crowd. Plus I'm in charge of traffic control. I was standing about fifty yards south of the speakers' platform. There must've been eight or ten shots. High-powered rifle, I'd say. Rapid-fire, too, so it was a semiautomatic. Had to be." He paused, drawing a deep breath. His voice had slipped into a high, unprofessional falsetto. "I saw one of the victims go down," he continued more deliberately. "She bucked back three feet. She was really hit, you know? So like I say, it's a powerful gun."

"Is anyone in custody?"

"Not that I know of." He pointed to the library. "The way it looked, the suspect had to've been firing from that direction. I mean, the way the victims fell, it's *got* to be."

"Is he in the library, you mean?"

He shrugged his beefy shoulders, snapping and unsnapping his holster strap as his gaze balefully traversed the plaza. "Christ, I don't know. The communications are piss-poor. I don't even know if I'm supposed to be in charge."

"Don't worry about it. I'm in charge now. Stand by, will you?" I turned toward Canelli. He stood only a step from my elbow, so that I brushed against him. He extended the walkie-talkie toward me with an oddly tentative gesture, as if he were afraid to antagonize me. "They're coming in on channel two, Lieutenant."

"Good." I got back on the roof of the car, then reached down for the radio. "This is Lieutenant Hastings. I want the men who are assisting the stewards to stay with them until the ambulances clear the area." I paused long enough to hear a few scattered acknowledgments of the order. "I'm in charge," I continued. "I'm at the corner of Larkin and McAllister, standing on top of a black-and-white. Has anyone seen a suspect?"

Scattered replies, all negative.

"Where did the shots come from? Which direction? Which building? Sound off."

The haphazard consensus was plain: the library. It had to be the library.

"Are all the exits from the building covered?"

Yes. Double-covered. Triple-covered. And men were inside. Four, five inspectors, at least.

I next asked for a precise time on the shooting. It averaged out to 1:22 P.M. Glancing at my watch, I made it seven min-

14

utes ago. "Is there anyone inside the library on this net?" I asked. Silence.

"All right. I'm proceeding to the front steps of the library." As I said it, the knot of officers standing on the library steps stood a little straighter. Two or three of them looked toward me. I slid to the ground again and handed the radio to Canelli, at the same time brushing off my suit. "You stay here," I ordered. "Keep Lieutenant Friedman informed. Tell him we've got all the personnel we need—for now, at least. Except for maybe a couple of sharpshooters."

"Yessir."

"Can you come with me, Dwight?"

Hanley nodded. "There're about four traffic sergeants here, at least," he said sourly. "Everyone's in everyone else's way."

"Let's go, then."

As we walked to the library steps, the first of the ambulances was getting under way, escorted by a pair of motorcycle officers. That would be the governor, I thought as I walked. I wondered whether he was dead, or dying. I'd never liked either him or his politics. Oddly, I realized that I felt resentful of the publicity he was getting.

As I mounted the library steps, I saw Sergeant Jerry Markham, from my own squad, emerging from one pair of the library's carved bronze doors. He was flanked by Dave Pass, from Bunco, and a new inspector on the vice squad. Markham, I knew, was off duty for three days. He was dressed casually in a poplin jacket and corduroy slacks. At age thirty, slim and handsome, he looked like a graduate student.

The three inspectors were closely followed by two women, one in her twenties, the other middle-aged. The women walked as though they were seeking safety in the officer's wake, staying close behind. The older woman's eyes darted uneasily toward the plaza; she was frightened.

Markham angled down to meet us, descending the broad stairs with an easy, graceful stride. As he approached, I could see the shadow of displeasure plain on Markham's handsome, arrogant face. Until that moment, he'd probably been the ranking officer on the scene.

The five of us formed a loose circle. The two women stopped a few steps away, whispering together. The original group of uniformed officers remained as before, awaiting orders. I glanced at the two women. The younger was frowning at her timid companion, speaking to her in a low, exasperated voice.

"What's the story?" I asked Markham.

He turned deliberately toward the library, squinting in the pale winter sunshine. He moved as if he were posing for a publicity picture. Raising his right arm, he pointed to a pair of small ornamental windows placed just above the building's massive Grecian lintel.

"The shots came from up there. There're shell cases all over the place. Thirty caliber, M-1. It's a dead-storage area—a kind of a loft. It's dusty, so you can see where he walked."

"Did you post someone up there to secure the area for the lab?"

"Certainly," he answered brusquely. Markham resented obvious questions, however necessary. He gestured toward the two women, speaking in a lowered voice. "The younger woman saw someone who looked Mexican go up the stairs leading to the loft. It was about twenty minutes ago—about ten minutes before the shooting. He was bareheaded, with a dark complexion. His hair is kind of scraggly, she says, and grows down to his collar. He's in his early twenties. And she's a pretty good witness, so I believe her. She's cool. The subject was wearing a blue gabardine topcoat that she thinks was dirty and ripped in spots. And—" He paused momentarily, for emphasis. "And she says he was climbing the stairs like he had a bad leg. Which could've been the rifle, under his coat."

"What about the other woman?"

"She saw him come down, right after the shooting. And he was in a hurry, she said—and still walking awkwardly, hopping down the stairs. So I figure we got at least a tentative make."

16

"Did anyone inside see him leave the building?"

"So far, no."

"Where does the stairway lead?"

"It goes from the top of the building to the basement. Five stories, altogether. It's used mostly by employees, but customers can use it, too—except that most of them don't. They either use the elevators or the main staircase."

"So if he's still in the building," I said, "he could be anywhere."

"Yes. And that building'll be a bitch to search, believe me."

I called for a walkie-talkie, and gestured for the uniformed men to join us. Using the radio, I described the suspect, asking if anyone had seen him leaving the library. For a few moments I got no response.

Then: "This is Bartham, Lieutenant. Traffic. I'm at the back of the library building, covering the tradesmen's entrance. And a bystander says that he saw the man you describe entering a blue two-door sedan. The witness didn't say anything about a limp, but the rest fits. And the time is about right."

"Is the witness there?"

"Yessir. He's with my partner."

"All right. Hold on to him. And see if you can get any more information on the subject's car, plus the direction it took."

"Yessir. I'm trying."

"Stay in the net."

"Yessir."

"Did you get that, Canelli?" I asked.

"I sure did, Lieutenant," came Canelli's voice.

"All right. Relay it to Lieutenant Friedman. He'll put it on the air. Tell him we're trying for supplemental information."

"Right."

I lowered the radio and turned toward the plaza. The last of the ambulances was leaving; the crowd was beginning to disperse. When the bloodied bodies disappeared, so did the rubberneckers.

I turned to Dave Pass and the vice inspector, whose name I still couldn't remember. "You men had better secure the speakers' platform for the lab crew. They should be here in ten minutes or so. Keep the four patrolmen with you, on the platform. But don't let them screw up the evidence."

Nodding, they moved off together.

I switched on the walkie-talkie, ordering that traffic be allowed to move. Next I instructed the officers clearing the plaza to finish their job, then stand by for further orders. Finally I turned to Markham. "We're going to have to search the library," I said, eying the Grecian monolith. "We can't assume that he escaped. Not yet."

Markham nodded, also surveying the library with a calm, coldly calculating stare. "What about the people inside?" he asked.

"How many customers would you say there are?"

He shrugged. "Maybe a hundred. I don't know. I wasn't counting." The tone of his voice deprecated the question's relevance. He was regarding me with a kind of amused, insolent tolerance.

"And probably thirty or forty staff." As I said it, I glanced thoughtfully around. We had at least sixty men on the scene, many of them merely awaiting orders. With that much manpower, we could do the screening job in a half-hour, no problem.

"I think," I said slowly, "that we're going to take everyone's name as we let them through. You set it up. We'll—"

"Lieutenant Hastings." Someone held out a walkie-talkie. "It's Bartham again. From the service entrance."

As I took the radio, I heard Bartham's voice saying, ". . . three witnesses who all say that it was a six- or seven-year-old American compact car, either a Nova or a Valiant. They can't agree on the make. But the car was beat up, they say, with a dented right front fender, except that some say it was the left. The body was rusted. And the driver was acting suspiciously, too—driving erratically, and in a hurry to leave the area."

"Have you got that, Canelli?"

"Yes, Lieutenant."

"Get it to Friedman. I'll be with you in a minute."

"Yessir."

18

I handed the walkie-talkie to a uniformed man, and turned to Markham. Ignoring his sardonic, elaborately resigned sigh, I ordered Markham to begin systematically clearing the building, screening everyone as they came out, holding only those who either acted suspiciously or couldn't identify themselves. There was, after all, always the possibility of an accomplice. Then, cutting off Markham's protest, I turned away, announcing that I wanted to speak with Friedman.

As I approached the black-and-white car, I saw Canelli beckoning urgently. I ran the last hundred feet. Canelli was standing beside the car.

"They might have him spotted, Lieutenant. There's a six-year-old Valiant proceeding south on Guerrero. Everything checks out."

I grabbed his walkie-talkie, telling Canelli to get our car, fast, and pick me up. Then, speaking into the radio, I ordered Markham to take over at the scene, proceeding as I'd ordered, and reporting to Friedman, on Tach Seven.

Four

I slammed the door, motioning for Canelli to turn west on McAllister. I decided to proceed code two: red light, no siren.

"Anything?" I asked.

Canelli nodded, blinking as he concentrated on the road ahead. "He's still on Guerrero. He—"

"Inspectors Eleven." It was Friedman's voice.

I grabbed the mike, acknowledging the call.

"What's your position, Frank?"

"We're on McAllister, proceeding— *Hey,*" I said sharply to Canelli, "don't turn here. There's construction on Market Street, for God's sake."

Canelli's sidelong look was reproachful as he straightened the car.

"We'll be on Guerrero in a minute or so," I said into the mike. "We—"

"Blue Valiant sedan is accelerating, Lieutenant Friedman," a strange voice cut in. "He's starting to run, I think."

"What's his position?" Friedman asked curtly.

"Guerrero and Nineteenth, still traveling south. But he's accelerating, like I said." I thought I could recognize the voice as Jack Drager's, from the General Works Detail. Good, I thought. The pursuing car would be unmarked.

"Have we got anyone paralleling the suspect?" Friedman asked urgently. "He's heading toward the freeway. We've only got fifteen blocks to stop him."

"This is Unit 607," someone said. "We're at Dolores and Sixteenth, paralleling him."

"Speed up," Friedman ordered. "But handle code two. No sirens."

We were crossing Market Street, against the light. As Canelli swung close behind a streetcar, a Porsche bore down on us fast from the right. With brakes locked, the Porsche was swinging broadside. I caught a momentary glimpse of a wide-eyed, bearded driver. His mouth was open wide, as if he were shouting. He would hit us on my side. I braced my knees, ducking my head between my shoulders, hands pressed to the instrument panel, elbows locked. I felt our car lurch sharply to the left; I could hear the Porsche's tire-shriek, close beside me. We were headed directly for a traffic island. As we struck the island's curb, Canelli wrenched the wheel to the right. With our engine roaring, we were clear, swinging into Guerrero.

". . . on Valencia and Twenty-second." It was a new voice. Automatically, I was visualizing the pursuit pattern: Drager was on Guerrero, two blocks behind the suspect. Black-and-white cars were in good position on both Valencia and Dolores, running even with the suspect. My car was bringing up the rear, closing fast. When Friedman got the two black-and-whites far enough ahead, he'd order an intersection blocked. We'd . . .

"Where are you, Drager?" Friedman was asking.

"We're at Twenty-first," came Drager's tight voice.

"Is he still accelerating?"

"He's going about forty. I don't know whether he's spooked, or just picking up speed. I can't decide."

"All right," Friedman said calmly, "we've got everyone in position. Let's block him at Army Street. That's the last chance to—"

"*Hey,*" Drager's voice interrupted, "he's taking a hard left, at Alvarado. He's jumped the divider."

"All right, that's good," Friedman said, his voice still slow and deliberate. "He can't make the freeway now. Let's get that unit on Valencia Street U-turned. Maybe we can stop him at—"

"He's pulling up," Drager said excitedly. "He's stopped between Guerrero and San Jose."

"All pursuing units, converge on that location," Friedman ordered. "Acknowledge."

Four units responded. I acknowledged last: "We're at Guerrero and Fourteenth, Pete. We'll be there shortly."

"All right, Frank. Take over. I'll stand by."

"Roger. This is Lieutenant Hastings. What's he doing, Drager?"

"Nothing. He's just sitting in his car. He's bent over in the seat, but I can't see what he's doing. Shall we try to take him?"

"No. Sit tight. Just keep me—"

"He's getting out of the car, Lieutenant. He's—Jesus, he's our boy, all right. He's got a rifle. It's . . ." Drager hesitated. Now his voice sounded awed. "It's an M-1, I think. A Garand, for God's sake. He—"

". . . turning into San Jose," a second voice said. "We can—"

"*Wait* a minute," I interrupted loudly. "I don't want to hear from anyone but Drager. All other units, proceed to the suspect's location, code two. Use extreme care. Repeat: extreme care. The suspect is armed. Seal off the block. Take cover. I don't want—"

"Look out, black-and-white!" Drager shouted. "He sees you, at the far end of the block. He— *Watch it!*"

I heard the sound of shots: three shots, rapid-fire. I flicked on the siren. "Hit it, Canelli."

"Yessir." The car surged forward, careening around a huge moving van, missing a wildly wobbling bicyclist by less than a foot.

". . . running into a building," Drager was saying. "He's inside. I can't see him now. He's gone inside a two-story private dwelling."

I tried to keep my voice calm as I asked, "What's the address of the building?"

"One sixty-seven Alvarado."

"All right. I want you and your partner to cover the back of that building, Drager. Right now. Have you got a walkie-talkie and a shotgun?"

"Yessir."

"Okay. Tune to channel one. We'll be on the scene any second now." I glanced at the street signs. We were at Twenty-first Street, three blocks from Alvarado. "Take off, Drager. Don't let him get out the back way."

"Yessir. Clear."

"How many other units are on the scene now?" I asked.

"Four," someone said. Another voice answered, "Five."

"Whoever said 'four,' I want that team to help Inspector Drager cover the back. Understood?"

"Yessir. We're on our way."

"Everyone else, take cover," I ordered. "Keep the civilians back. Check the roofs. We're almost there."

A pair of motorcycle officers curved into Guerrero just ahead—as if they were escorting us. Alvarado was next. The motorcycles braked, hopped up on the divider, then down. We followed, too fast. As our car rocked violently, striking the divider, I fleetingly wondered about the tires and the tie rods. Everything held together. It was a short street, half the normal block length. I hurriedly counted four black-and-white cars, plus Drager's cruiser, plus ours. Other sirens sounded close by, converging.

"Get as close as you can," I ordered Canelli. And into the open mike: "Pete."

"Yes. It sounds good."

"I don't need any more personnel. Not now, anyhow."

"Roger. How're you going to proceed?"

Canelli was pulling to a jolting stop almost directly opposite 167 Alvarado. It was a dingy, paint-peeling, two-flat building with an ordinary peaked roof. The building was a row house, sharing a common wall with the house on either side. The suspect couldn't escape over the roofs without being seen—and shot.

"If the back is covered," I said into the mike, "he's bottled up. He's got nowhere to go. We'll take it slow and easy. We can probably smoke him out."

"Do you want a sharpshooter?" Friedman asked. "There's one at the Civic Center."

"All right, send him over. How's the governor?"

"I haven't heard. Shall I come over there?"

"No. I—"

A woman's figure was suddenly running past our car, making for the white frame house. She ran grotesquely—as if she'd been wounded—and was staggering, about to pitch headlong onto the pavement. Her outstretched arms were raised wide; her graying hair blew behind her as she ran. Her skin was brown; she was Chicano. Her mouth gaped as she gasped desperately for breath. Her eyes were wild and rolling.

"Cover me, Canelli. Put the word out: cover me." I threw open the car's door, at the same time drawing my revolver. The woman was crossing the far sidewalk, reeling toward the house's twin front doors. She half fell, then caught herself. She was screaming, "Carlos, Carlos!" As I reached the sidewalk, she hurled herself against the right-hand door, beating her fists against the panels. As I sprinted the last few yards, I glanced up, searching the second-story windows for the movement of a rifle barrel. Nothing. Now the woman was fumbling wildly at the doorknob, using both hands. She was still screaming, "Carlos!" Just the single word, over and over.

As she wrenched open the door, my last stride carried me onto the small porch. I was safe; the porch roof protected me—and the woman. The door was swinging open. Behind her now, I circled her thick waist with both arms, still gripping my revolver in my right hand. Bracing my legs, I pivoted, throwing my weight against the woman's forward momentum. She was too heavy for me: a gross, awkward bulk, falling away. We were tumbling to-

24

gether into a small, shabby entryway. Cursing, I released her waist. I threw her flat against the inside wall, protecting her from fire from down the stairway. With my left forearm jammed across her chest, pinning her to the wall, I quickly looked up the stairway. Nothing stirred. But if he came down the stairs firing the M-1, I'd be in trouble, with only a pistol.

"Mi niño," she was screaming. Now I could feel her sagging against me. Her eyes were rolling up. She was going into shock.

*"Mi niño—*my boy."

"You're his mother?" I hissed into her brown peasant's face.

"Sí, sí. Su madre."

It was a hell of a time to conduct an interrogation in two languages. I glanced again up the stairway, exposing only half my face. It was still clear.

"What's his name?" I asked the wild-eyed woman. "His full name. What's his full name?"

"Carlos. Carlos Ramirez." Her voice was a whisper now. Her mouth was gaping. She was sinking slowly, sliding down the wall. I let her slide into a splay-legged sitting position, crouching above her.

"Do you live upstairs, Mrs. Ramirez?"

She slowly shook her head. "It's Angela," she whispered. "Upstairs. Angela. He's with her, the *mujerzuela*. She made him do it. Angela." Her head fell forward on her chest. Her eyes were blank; her mouth gaped.

Mujerzuela. Slut.

I cupped my left hand beneath her chin, raising her head. "Which apartment, Mrs. Ramirez? Which apartment is hers? Tell me. Then I'll get help for you. But you have to tell me."

"You—you will kill him. *Asesinar* him."

"No, Mrs. Ramirez. We aren't murderers."

Her lips were gray, her eyes half closed. *"Detras de,"* she muttered.

The back.

Cautiously, I pulled the front door open. I could just see Canelli, crouched behind our cruiser. To his right, the riot wagon was pulling up, probably diverted from the Civic Center. The wagon carried emergency gear: respirators, stretchers, everything.

"Canelli," I called softly.

"Yessir."

"Bring three men, a stretcher, a shotgun and a walkie-talkie. Quick."

I watched him moving awkwardly from car to car, bent double. In thirty seconds the team was ready, all of them crouched down behind our cruiser, the closest. Each of the four men was lifting his face, stealing a last fleeting look at the upstairs windows. I saw Canelli swallow slowly. Beside me, Ramirez' mother was moaning, retching.

"All right," I called. *"Now."*

The four men broke for the porch, all of them running crouched, zigzagging. Canelli carried his revolver in one hand, a walkie-talkie in the other. The patrolman with the rolled-up stretcher reached the porch first. Canelli was next. The third man held a shotgun. Holstering my pistol, I beckoned for the shotgun. I pulled the slide slightly back, checking on the cartridge in the chamber. I clicked off the safety, then stepped to my right, facing directly up the stairway, shotgun ready.

"All right," I said softly. "I'll cover you. I want two of you to take the woman out of here on the stretcher. Canelli, you stay here. The odd man, too. I think the suspect is in the back apartment, so there's no problem—yet." I spoke over my shoulder, keeping the shotgun trained on the upstairs landing, ready.

In a moment, the two officers were gone, staggering under the woman's weight. Upstairs, nothing stirred. I drew a long, slow breath, again speaking over my shoulder: "Get Drager on the radio, Canelli."

"Yessir." A brief pause. Then: "I've got him, Lieutenant."

"Hold the radio up so I can hear," I said. And sidelong into the mike: "Drager?"

"Yes, Lieutenant."

26

"How's it look back there?"

"All quiet, Lieutenant."

"Is there any means of getting out the back way from the upstairs flat?"

"Yessir. There's an outside stairway."

"Do you think the suspect could've gotten out and down those stairs before you got there?"

"I don't see how, Lieutenant."

"Okay, then he's still up there. Keep your eyes open. He could be coming your way."

"Yessir."

"How many men are with you?"

"Three."

"Could you get a gas grenade in one of the upstairs windows, do you think?"

"Probably."

"All right. The riot wagon's here. They'll get a grenade launcher to you. When you've got it, stand by. Let me know when you're in position to get a canister inside. But keep your head down, meanwhile. Don't forget, he's got an automatic rifle. An M-1."

I heard him half snicker. "Don't worry."

I listened to the walkie-talkie for a moment, until I was sure that a grenade launcher was on its way. The process seemed to take longer than necessary, but was probably accomplished in less than a minute. When I heard Drager confirming that he had the launcher and was ready, I told him to stand by, then handed the radio to Canelli.

"All right," I whispered, "let's see what we've got. You two men cover me. But stay well behind me on the stairs, in case we want to get out quick."

Slowly, step by creaking step, I began climbing the narrow staircase. As my head came above the level of the upstairs hallway floor, I had a clear view of two doors, apparently leading to two separate apartments, front and rear. Both doors were closed. I could hear nothing.

Had he slipped away—out the back, before Drager could intercept him? Had he climbed over the roofs? I stood perfectly still, my forefinger touching my lips, listening.

From the rear apartment came the faint sound of voices.

Silently, I handed the shotgun to the patrolman, gesturing for him to train the gun on the rear doorway. "The safety's off," I whispered, "and there's a round in the chamber. So watch it."

He nodded. I held his eye for a last long, hard moment. He looked young—and nervous. He would be behind me with a gun that could blow my leg off at close range.

"Watch it," I repeated. "Give me a chance to drop before you fire."

Again he nodded, swallowing hard. I turned away from him, drawing my revolver as I climbed the last four stairs. Now I could plainly hear voices, speaking in low, fierce undertones. I inched closer to the apartment door until I stood with my ear against the panel. My revolver came up even with my chin. Looking at the gun, I realized that I'd forgotten to draw back the hammer. If I had to shoot, I'd be shooting double-action, never accurate. But I didn't want to risk two hammer-clicks.

Someone inside was saying, *"Take* her, for Christ's sake. She's nothing to me. If you want her, *take* her. But don't shoot me. She—she's nothing to me. *Nothing.* I was going to move out of here. I swear it. This weekend, I was going to move. I been just —just hanging around until I got a little money. But, hell, me and her, we're just—just shacked up for a little while. It's no big deal. We just—"

"You're a dirty, crawling, lying bastard. You—"

"Don't. Please, please don't." The voice was fear-choked, hardly audible. "I—I'll do anything you want. But please don't—"

"Shut up."

"All right. I'll shut up. But I—"

"I warn you: don't talk. Another word, and I'll shoot you. I've shot others today—many others." The voice was viciously accented with a soft, menacing Spanish sibilance.

For a moment, there was silence. Then I could hear the accented voice say: "I killed them all. Four, five people. They all were falling, slipping in each other's blood. The governor, when he died, was reaching up, like he was grabbing for the sky. I could see how his fingers were crooked. His hand looked like a claw—like a chicken's claw. I—" Laughter suddenly burbled madly. "A chicken. Did I say a chicken?"

"Yes," the other voice answered eagerly. "You said—"

"*Shut up.*" It was a low, hysterical scream-whisper. "I *told* you, shut up."

"All right, Ramirez. Jesus, I—"

"When is Angela coming?"

"I—I already told you, I don't know where she went. I swear it. She went shopping, I think. Just shopping. I—"

"Maybe I won't kill you until she gets back. I think maybe I won't. And then, maybe, I'll kill you both. What do you think of that, you crawling bastard?"

"No, no. Please, Ramirez. You can't. You—"

"For me, who have killed the governor, it don't matter. It's all the same now. It—" The hysterical laughter erupted again.

Slowly I backed down the stairway, carefully feeling for each step, motioning the two men down behind me. At the downstairs landing, I stopped them. I took the shotgun from the patrolman.

"Go get us three gas masks," I ordered.

"Yessir." He turned quickly away.

I set the shotgun's safety, then turned to Canelli. I reached for the radio. "Drager?"

"Yessir."

"See anything?"

"No."

"Are you ready with the gas?"

"Yessir."

"You've got to make the first shot good. I don't think he'll stand still for number two. He's irrational, and he's got a hostage in there."

"I'll do my best."

The patrolman was back with three gas masks.

"What's your name?" I asked him, taking my mask.

"Parker, sir."

"Well, you take the walkie-talkie, Parker. Wait down here, in the entryway. When I give you the signal—when I nod—tell Drager to shoot the gas. Then you put on your mask. But stay down here. I don't want you on the stairway."

He nodded, a little shakily. He'd probably never faced a gun before.

I slipped on the mask, tested it, then picked up the shotgun. Pointing the shotgun up the stairs. I clicked off the safety. I looked over my shoulder at Canelli, lifting my head inquiringly up the stairs. Canelli nodded. He was perspiring heavily.

Once more I began slowly climbing the staircase. This time I stopped two steps from the top, giving myself room to swing the shotgun. I motioned for Canelli to stop three steps down from me, with his head just above the level of the hallway. He could fire through the banister spokes. Canelli cocked his revolver. He was ready. He seemed steady, cool. I looked down to Parker, and nodded. I heard him order the gas.

Almost immediately I heard the sound of shattering glass, followed by the angry hiss of the C.S. gas. I nodded to Canelli. He returned the nod. I watched my left hand tightening on the shotgun's forestock. Inside my gas mask, perspiration was stinging my face. In a moment, the faceplate would begin to fog. I'd have to . . .

"*No—no!*" a voice screamed from inside. "*Jesus, no!*" The apartment door shuddered, struck a sharp, sudden blow. The doorknob was turning; the door was coming open. I crouched down behind the riot gun. I . . .

A shot cracked; splinters flew from the door, close to the floor. Someone screamed. The door came fully open. A large man, blond, tumbled out into the hallway. He wore only undershorts. Blood streaked his thigh. His eyes were streaming. He screamed incoherently as he staggered to his feet. His arms were thrown wide with the wild, desperate groping of a blind man. From inside the apartment came three quick shots, then a fourth. Plaster exploded on the hallway ceiling; two holes appeared in the front apartment's door. The blond man screamed again as he lurched against the flimsy railing. For an instant the railing held the man's bulk. Then, slow-motion-splintering, the banister was coming down. The man was falling. His gangle-limbed body struck Canelli, hunched against the wall. He was tumbling down the stairs, smearing blood on the dingy paint of the side wall. Below, Parker's mask-muffled exclamation seemed oddly petulant.

I returned my eyes to the still-open door, with its single splintered panel. The sound of coughing came from inside the apartment. Yellow, floor-clinging tendrils of C.S. gas were eddying out into the hallway. They were . . .

A shot cracked out—a single shot. Then nothing.

I cleared my throat. "Throw the gun out, Ramirez. Right now. Then come out with your hands on top of your head."

Nothing stirred. Then another spasm of coughing erupted. The edges of my faceplate were fogging. Holding the shotgun with my right hand, I used my left hand to lift the bottom of my gas mask. The acrid smell of gas stung my nostrils. I replaced the mask, settling it in place. I'd have to . . .

The muzzle of a rifle was sliding into view, moving slowly through the open door.

Crouching lower, I trained my shotgun waist high. Now the rifle's handstock was visible, and a white-knuckled brown hand. Next came the dirty blue gabardine sleeve of a raincoat. I was holding my breath, blinking my eyes against the sudden sting of sweat. A foot slowly appeared—a leg. My finger was taking up the trigger-slack. Another foot followed the first, then the suspect's full figure, topcoat-clad, just as he'd been described. Ramirez' swarthy face was tear-streaked. His eyes were tightly closed. He held the rifle parallel to the floor, probing before him as he moved slowly forward. He was coughing now, choking. But still he moved inexorably ahead, blindly making for the door of the front apartment.

If I called on him to surrender, would he whirl toward the sound of my voice, firing his semiautomatic rifle as he turned?

At the spoke-splintered gap in the banister he hesitated. The gas still choked him; he was still blinded by his tears. Again he moved forward, sliding his feet clumsily across the tattered hallway carpet. What would he do when the muzzle of the rifle touched something?

The question, unanswered, decided me. I took the last two steps quickly. I was behind the suspect, pacing with him. The muzzle of my gun pointed directly at the small of his back. At that range, the buckshot blast would cut him in two. Tiptoing, I closed the distance between us. Now his gun was within three feet of the opposite door. Two feet. I stepped quickly forward, swinging the shotgun in a short, vicious arc. The wooden stock crashed into Ramirez' head. I heard the sodden, melon-thumped sound of the wood striking flesh, felt the shock in my arms and shoulders. His legs slowly buckled; the big military rifle fell heavily to the floor. With a long, soft sigh, Ramirez sunk slowly to his knees, swayed for a moment, then suddenly toppled forward.

Five

I slumped into the passenger's seat of the cruiser, and reached for the mike. The effort seemed enormous.

"This is Lieutenant Hastings," I said. As I spoke, Canelli got behind the wheel, grunting heavily.

"You got him, eh?" Friedman said. "Nice going. The governor, by the way, is expected to live. In fact, all of the victims—all four of them—are expected to live. How about the hostage?"

"He'll live, too. He's just shot in the leg."

"How about Ramirez?"

"He's still unconscious. He might have a concussion, but I don't think his skull is fractured."

"You sound tired," Friedman said.

"I *am* tired."

"Are you going to check out that Hoffman Street thing, or shall I tell Culligan to handle it?"

"Is he still waiting for me?"

"Sure. It's only been forty-five minutes, you know, since I first called you. Time passes fast when you're busy."

I snorted, then shrugged. "I may as well check it out. It's less than a mile from here. I'll send Canelli downtown, to keep the chain of evidence."

"Roger. Anything else?"

"No."

"You done good, Lieutenant. Oh, by the way, your friend Ann Haywood called—my favorite schoolmarm. She phoned you, and Communications put her through because they know her. Anyhow, she somehow got plugged into Tach Seven, for God's sake, and found out that you were busy shooting it out with a bad guy. So do you want me to tell her you're okay?"

"She was in the *net?*" It was an outrageous possibility.

"Don't try to cope with it, Lieutenant. These things happen. Shall I call her, or not?"

Ann . . .

"All right, thanks."

"You're welcome. I'll see you in a couple of hours, eh?"

"Roger."

I sank back in the seat, watching the tangle of official cars begin to clear the area. The ambulances were just pulling away.

Forty-five minutes . . .

Momentarily I closed my eyes, drawing a long, deep breath. "Did you order a squad car to stand by here?" I asked Canelli.

"Yessir."

"You'll have to get a ride down to the Hall. Report to Lieutenant Friedman."

"Right." He hesitated, then said, "Jeeze, it hasn't even been an hour since we left the Hall. I can't believe it. Man, I feel like I been through a war, or something. Is that the way you feel, Lieutenant?"

"That's right, Canelli. That's the way I feel." I still lay back against the seat, again allowing my eyes to close.

"You know," Canelli said softly, "when I was crouched down there in that stairway, waiting for Ramirez to come out, I started wondering how the hell I *got* there—what I was *doing* there. I mean—" He paused. "I mean, it just didn't seem possible that it was me, waiting there to maybe kill somebody. Know what I mean, Lieutenant?"

I opened my eyes. "This is a tough business, Canelli. Didn't they tell you that at the academy?"

"Yeah. But hearing it's one thing. Doing it's something else."

"You'll be all right, Canelli. You aren't the best driver in the world. But I feel safe with you backing me up. And that's what it's all about—the crunch."

"Well, thanks, Lieutenant. Thanks a lot." His voice revealed both surprise and pleasure.

For a long, tired moment we sat in silence. Finally Canelli asked, "How'd you get to be a cop, Lieutenant? I mean, you been to college, and everything. And you even played pro football, I know. So . . ." He lapsed into a tentative, hopeful silence.

To myself, I smiled. "I got in through pull, Canelli. Captain Kreiger and I played football together at Stanford. But he was smarter than I was. He majored in police science, and then got into police work after college. I majored in football, although they called it business administration. So when my so-called football career ran out and my marriage went sour, I came back to San Francisco. And"—I shrugged—"and when Kreiger said that he could help me get into the academy, I went for it. I was the oldest rookie in my class. Luckily, though, I was in good shape. Physically, at least." I sat straighter, glancing up and down the block. Only three cars remained, waiting for dispatch.

I said again, "You'd better catch yourself a ride to the Hall, Canelli. You and I are the chain of evidence. And I won't be downtown for an hour or so."

"Oh. Yeah." He hastily got out of the car, then turned back, as if he were about to say something. Finally he half saluted, smiled uncertainly, and called to a black-and-white car.

I glanced at my watch. If Culligan had waited this long, I decided, he could wait a few minutes more. Again I settled back in the seat, allowing my eyes to close. At forty-three years of age, I'd finally learned the value of catnaps.

The oldest rookie in my class . . .

I could talk about it now—smile about it.

But I still couldn't talk about failure. That would take another ten years—another decade. Canelli had sensed something missing in my story—some secret, essential component that would make the sum total credible. He probably didn't suspect, though, that the component's label was failure.

The failure component . . .

I'd coined a half-catchy phrase: Dale Carnegie, turned mockingly around. How to succeed as a policeman without wanting to be a policeman—or anything else, really.

Yet I'd wanted to play football. I'd tried hard. For a few years, I probably had the potential.

But I'd married an heiress: a tawny, predatory blonde, with a balding, predatory father. Jason Carlson, Detroit industrialist. When the Lions finally cut me loose, Jason had found a P.R. spot for me in his "organization." He never referred to his business as a foundry. It was "the organization." The executives were "team members."

But the P.R. man, I soon discovered, was merely the team greeter, the golf partner, the drinking buddy, the chauffeur. Even the procurer, if the customers were horny enough—and important enough. Another "team member" took care of the publicity releases and the bad press notices. I took care of the customers' libidos. The high-level pimping had been the final phase of my P.R. career, capping the grisly climax. By that time, in the line of duty, my cocktail hour began at noon and seemed to have no end. My wife, meanwhile, had found other drinking companions. My children had become . . .

"Lieutenant Hastings." Startled, I straightened, opening my eyes, blinking. It was the walkie-talkie, lying on the seat beside me.

"What is it?" I looked toward the last remaining squad car, parked across the street, directly in front of the white frame house. This car would remain, securing the area.

A dark, dumpy girl stood beside the squad car. "I've got Angela

Ortega here, Lieutenant. The occupant of the apartment. Do you want to talk with her?"

"All right. Send her over." I got out of the car, moving heavily. The girl was crossing the street toward me. She walked with a slow, dragging reluctance. I opened my car's rear door and motioned her into the back seat. She hesitated, searching my face with dark, darting eyes. Her arms were stiff at her sides, fists clenched.

"Get in," I said. "Nobody's going to hurt you. I just want to ask you a few questions."

She edged past me, sliding into the car. She sat in the far corner of the seat, turned to face me. She'd been in a police car before.

"Do you know Carlos Ramirez?" I asked.

"*Sí. Yo le conozco.*"

"Talk English, Miss Ortega," I said sharply. "If you cooperate, this won't take long. If you don't . . ." I let it go unfinished.

"Yeah," she said heavily. "Yeah, I know him. Is he—" Her eyes widened. "Jesus. Is he the one who—who—"

"That's right," I said. "He's the one. And his mother said that it's your fault—that he did it because of you. You made him do it, she said."

"*Me?*" She gaped. "*Qué pasa*—What'd you mean, me?" As she asked the question, her face registered first shock, then surprise, finally a kind of slack, speculative puzzlement. "What'd you mean?" she repeated, watching me avidly. "I'm not even here. All day long, man, I been downtown. I don' come here all day. So you can't say I—"

"What's your connection with Carlos Ramirez, Miss Ortega?"

She frowned. "What'd you mean? What 'connection'?"

"Were you lovers? Is that it?"

Her lip curled. "Carlos, he's a—a nothing. Nobody. He never talks, never does nothing. He—he's—" Her mouth worked as she struggled for the word. "He's *demente,*" she said finally. She tapped at her forehead.

"Crazy, you mean?"

"*Nada*—no. Not crazy, so much. Just strange. He never does nothing, like I said. He just sits, man, and talks to himself sometimes. He's twenty, but he's a boy. Twelve. Thirteen." She raised her palms, shrugging elaborately.

I looked her over, taking my time. Her face was round and lumpish, her eyes lusterless, her mouth slack. Her black hair fell in untidy tangles to her shoulders. She wore skintight jeans and a tight turtleneck sweater. Her figure, like her face, was thick and gross.

"What about the man in your apartment, Miss Ortega? The blond man. What's his name?"

"Him?" I watched her expression change to one of dull-witted streetcorner guile. "You mean Frankie?"

I nodded. "The blond one. The one who's living with you."

"Yeah. Well, we're just"—she shrugged—"you know, man, we're just making it for a while. That's all."

"How old are you, Miss Ortega?"

"Twenty-five."

"Do you work?"

"Sure, I work. Every day. Except today, I mean. Today's my day off. Wednesdays. I'm a waitress, see?"

"Have you ever been arrested?"

"Aw, man—" She sullenly lowered her eyes. Affirmative.

"How many times have you and Carlos made love?"

The transparently crafty expression returned. "Man, I don' have to answer that. What'd you think, I'm *estúpido?*"

"I'm not accusing you of anything, Miss Ortega. But Carlos Ramirez tried to kill the governor. And it's my job to find out—"

"The governor?" Plainly, she couldn't comprehend it. *"El gobernador?"*

I nodded, watching her. Then I glanced at my watch.

Suddenly she laughed. Soon she was laughing uncontrollably. I let her finish. At last, choking and wiping at her eyes with the back of her hand, she said, *"Cristo,* Carlos was a boy, you know. Not a man. You know what I mean? He—he couldn't *do* it. Noth-

38

ing. But now he shoots the governor." She shook her head, still wiping at her mascara-smeared eyes. Then, blinking, she frowned, struck by a sudden thought.

"Hey," she said slowly, "what you say a minute ago—that it's my fault. You mean it's my fault about the governor? You don' mean Frankie? You mean the *governor?*"

"Maybe both, Miss Ortega. Maybe Carlos wanted to impress you—show you he was someone. So he tried to kill the governor."

"Hey." She was half-smiling, preening now. "Hey, you think so? You think that was it?" The slack, thick-lipped smile widened. "All I ever did with Carlos was—you know—tease him, because he couldn't do it. We jus'—fool around, you know? I let him fool around, once in a while. But I was just having fun. That's all I ever did—jus' have fun with him. A little teasing, you know? And he never say nothing. Jus' sorta smile when I tease him. Even last night. Jus' last night, while Frankie was working. But Carlos jus' smile, and don' say nothing."

I studied her for a last long moment, then deliberately reached across to open the door. "You can go upstairs now, Miss Ortega. But don't go anywhere. We'll want to talk to you again."

I watched her swagger off across the street in her skintight, buttocks-bulging jeans. Then I turned the ignition key, starting the engine. Culligan would be waiting at the Hoffman Street address. On my way, I'd order Angela picked up as a material witness.

Six

I parked a half-block from 436 Hoffman, and as I walked to the scene I assessed the neighborhood. Most of the houses were solid and substantial, built before 1920 and carefully maintained. Hoffman Street was in San Francisco's Noe Valley—traditionally a blue-collar district, more recently adopted by a scattering of long-haired young people and mod, with-it professional types, all of whom liked Noe Valley's solid, post-Victorian architecture and its views from the lower slopes of Twin Peaks. Noe Valley was acquiring an ethnic, nostalgic aura. As a consequence, property values were beginning to climb.

The building at 436 Hoffman had originally been a small corner store. Now its two plate-glass show windows were three-quarter frosted. Bright, psychedelic fabric showed above the frosting. The building's other windows, originally lighting upstairs living quarters, were curtained in a colorful hodgepodge of burlap, paisley prints and slatted bamboo. The building needed a coat of paint and numerous minor repairs. From outside appearances, the place could be a warren of hippie-style crash pads.

Recognizing me, the patrolman guarding the storefront apartment's front door came to attention. As he opened the door for me, I glanced briefly at the small knot of onlookers, mostly neighborhood children. It was a classic childhood tableau: kids of assorted sizes and shapes, dogs and wagons, bats and balls.

Inside, Culligan and John Tharp, the medical examiner, were seated together on a low, lumpy mattress that had been covered with bright orange corduroy and placed directly on the floor, to serve as a couch. As Tharp rose to his feet, he pointedly glanced at his watch. He was a small, humorless man with a perpetual frown and a pursed, petulant mouth.

"We were about to give you up," Tharp said acidly.

"I got delayed."

"Well, as far as I'm concerned, they can move the body." He picked up his satchel and hat, then stood squarely before me in a posture of brusque, peremptory expectation. He was required to wait until the officer in charge released him. His permission, plus mine, was necessary before the body could be moved.

Ignoring Tharp's fidgeting, I turned to Culligan. "Are the lab boys through?"

"Yes. Everything's dusted, everything's photographed and everything's outlined. So I let them all go. I mean—" As he hesitated, I nodded approval. There was no point in his detaining the technicians even though, by the book, I should have been the one to dismiss them.

"Where is it?" I asked.

Culligan pointed through a bead-bangled archway, leading into what had originally been a storeroom. Unconsciously holding my breath against the sickening, excremental stench of death, I parted the strings of beads and stepped through the archway.

It was a bedroom, wrecked. The body was tumbled into a two-foot space between the double bed and the wall. He lay on his right side, with his face jammed flat against the wall. His right arm was bent behind his back at an odd, shoulder-broken angle. His left arm lay along his side. His legs were extended full length, ankles peacefully crossed. A sizable smear of blood streaked the white-painted wall beside the bed. The front of his jacket was blood-caked, matching the smear on the wall. He'd probably struck the wall with his chest, then slid to the floor. Glancing around the room, I saw blood everywhere: puddled on the floor,

41

spattered on the walls, smeared on the furniture. By the look of it, he'd been stabbed in the heart.

I stepped through the bead strings, reentering the living room. Tharp was impatiently snapping and unsnapping the lock on his gleaming black satchel.

"What about it?" I asked Tharp.

"Well, of course, there isn't much I can say," he began defensively. "I mean, about all I could do was check the limb flexion. But just eyeballing it, I'd say he was stabbed repeatedly with a reasonably thin-bladed knife. I'd also say that he's been dead for twelve hours, at least. Beyond that, I can't really tell you much."

"Were there any bruises?"

"None that are visible. Aside from the multiple stab wounds concentrated in the abdomen, the only other injuries I can see are lacerations of the palms."

"As if he fought for the knife, you mean."

"Or was fending it off."

I nodded, and turned inquiringly to Culligan. "Anything else?"

Culligan shook his head. He was a tall, gaunt, thin-chested man with hollow cheeks and haggard, fatigue-smudged eyes. Culligan had a slatternly, abusive wife, a delinquent daughter and a duodenal ulcer. He was prematurely bald and prematurely stooped. Culligan said very little, but he was a shrewd, skillful detective, however taciturn. He knew that my question was perfunctory—that I was about to dismiss Tharp so that we could get down to business. Therefore, Culligan merely shook his head.

"Okay," I said to Tharp. "But get the autopsy to us as soon as possible, huh?" I glanced at the time. It was 2:45 P.M. "How about, say, ten o'clock tomorrow morning?"

Tharp shrugged peevishly. "I'll see what I can do." He turned toward the door. "Shall I send in the gurney?"

"Yes."

I followed the ambulance stewards into the bedroom, and watched them load the body on the gurney.

"I didn't check the right-hand pockets," Culligan said, "because of the way he was lying."

"Do it now. Go through everything. I'm your witness."

Culligan stepped forward impassively and began methodically going through the pockets, deftly turning the body from side to side. The feel of a corpse didn't seem to disturb him. Wryly, I wondered whether others thought the same of me.

When Culligan had finished, he took two Polaroid pictures of the victim's face, one picture for each of us. I stepped to the body, silently staring down into the dead face. Imagining the lolling mouth closed and the lusterless eyes animated, I figured he must have been good-looking. His face was lean and handsome—the face of a lady's man. His medium-brown hair was modishly razor-cut, his sideburns carefully trimmed to complement the with-it hair style. He was clean-shaven. His clothes were expensive. He wore an elaborately saddle-stitched leather jacket, flared slacks and eighty-dollar Wellington boots. His turtleneck shirt was rib-knit. Culligan was right. He didn't belong where he'd died.

"Got everything?" I asked Culligan.

Again he nodded. From the pinched look on Culligan's face, I knew that his ulcer was bothering him.

"Okay, take it away," I told the stewards. They deftly covered the body, securing the white plastic sheet with bands of black elastic. A moment later they were gone.

I turned to Culligan. "What'd you find in his pockets?"

He'd slipped everything into a large, clear-plastic evidence bag, which he silently handed to me. I saw a small stag-handled pocket-knife, a handful of silver coins and a neatly folded handkerchief.

"That's all?" I asked.

"That's all. No billfold or keys or correspondence."

"A goddamn John Doe."

"Looks like it."

"Anything else?"

He reached into his outside jacket pocket, carefully withdrawing a smaller bag. It contained an open switchblade knife. The handle and blade were caked with dried blood.

"Is that the murder weapon?"

He shrugged. "It could be."

I suppressed a smile. If Friedman was the garrulous one, and Canelli was the innocent and Markham the heavy, then Culligan was the silent one.

"Where'd you find it?" I asked.

"In a trash can about four doors down the block. Sigler found it."

"What's Sigler doing now?"

"He's checking out the neighbors. We still can't find anyone who heard anything last night."

"What else? Who discovered the body?"

"Nobody discovered the body," Culligan replied. "At least, no civilian. An anonymous phone tip came in at eleven fifteen A.M. today. The voice was disguised, according to Communications. It could have been either a man or a woman. It just said, 'Take a look inside the big apartment at 436 Hoffman.' So a radio car responded. The front door was latched, but unlocked. They just walked in. I got the call about noon. We were up in Miraloma Park, on that Thompson thing. So we came over."

"How about physical evidence?" As I asked the question, I began walking slowly through the apartment, to get a feel of the place. The layout was simply a living room, a small bedroom and an even smaller kitchen. The tiny bath was dark and dingy, just a toilet and a sheet-metal shower. A small door connected the kitchen to the rear service porch. The door was bolted and chained.

"There really isn't much physical evidence," Culligan was saying. "The back door is bolted, as you can see. There's no way anyone could get in through the windows. The front ones are solid plate glass. That leaves the windows in the bedroom and kitchen. And they're too small and too high. Plus they were latched, anyhow."

"So the murderer came in through the front door." We were back in the living room now. "Any jimmy marks?"

"No. But the murderer could already have been here, you know."

I nodded. "Either way, though, he must've left by the front door."

"Right."

"Who's the apartment belong to?"

"According to a girl who lives upstairs—her name is Judy Blake —the tenant is Diane Farley. Which might be a lead, because the vice squad's got a yellow sheet on her. I haven't seen it yet, though."

"Did you put out an A.P.B. on her?"

"I sure did."

"Is Diane Farley a hooker?" As I asked the question, I glanced around the apartment once more. It didn't look like a hooker's place.

Culligan shrugged. "I figured I'd wait till I got down to the Hall to pull her jacket, Lieutenant. The vice squad, you know, doesn't like to give that stuff out over the phone. They're getting harder to do business with all the time."

"What about this Judy Blake? What's her story?"

"She's pretty straight, I'd say. She says she's a graduate student at State College, and I believe her. She's a walking encyclopedia."

"Is she still here?"

"Yeah. I, ah, persuaded her to cut a class and stick around in case you wanted to talk to her."

I checked the time. "I'd better not. I have to get back to the Hall. Did you hear about the governor?"

"No."

"He got shot. A Chicano kid did it. With an M-1, if you can believe that."

"Did he kill the governor?"

"No. In fact, no one was killed." As I said it, I turned absently away, strolling through the apartment for a last look. In the kitchen, I noted the untidy stack of dirty dishes, the old, cheap stove and refrigerator, the stained and cracked linoleum on the floor.

The bedroom furnishings consisted only of a decrepit old-fashioned bureau with a clouded mirror, a double mattress covered with a peony-printed spread, and a rickety chair. The bedsprings were supported by four concrete blocks. The chair was laden with a woman's clothing. A small white shag rug, soaked with blood, was spread on the floor near the bed. The bedroom walls were covered with posters, most of them either erotic or hip—or both. A cork bulletin board was nailed to the wall beside the bureau. The cork was entirely covered with photographs, most of them eight-by-ten glossies. The subject was the same in each picture: a dark-haired girl in her twenties, with a good figure and a narrow, closed face. The photos were obviously the work of a professional photographer. In about half of them, the girl was nude. All of the poses, nude or not, were provocative.

"That," Culligan said, "is Diane Farley. Not bad, huh?"

I smiled. "If any of these pictures are missing, Culligan, I'll know where to look." I strode into the living room. An old-fashioned wind-up phonograph stood on a cut-down oak dining table. Two wicker chairs had been painted a gleaming white. A huge mound of pillows was piled on the mattress-cum-couch. In this room, the poster art was more restrained. In one corner a large rubber plant grew in a tarnished brass spittoon. The place had a with-it feeling, furnished for a far-out young person. I wondered whether she could be working her way through college by turning tricks. It happens.

"It looks like she's lived here for a while," I said thoughtfully.

"Yeah, she has."

"How many apartments are there in the building?"

"Four, besides this one. They're all small—just studios. There's one on this floor, and three upstairs."

"Where's Judy Blake's apartment?"

"Upstairs."

I glanced again at my watch. "It's after three. I'd better get downtown. You and Sigler keep at it, here. You don't have anything else that's hot, do you?"

He shrugged. "Not really. That Thompson thing isn't going anywhere."

"All right. If I have time, I'll check Diane Farley's rap sheet when I get to the hall. If it's anything heavy, I'll get back to you."

"Okay. See you, Lieutenant."

"Right. Good luck."

Seven

I'd just finished locking up the cruiser when I heard the first reporter's voice: "Hey, Lieutenant. Got a minute?" And the raucous, jostling pack was quickly on me, crowding me against the garage's concrete wall. Blinking against the flash bulbs, I looked down to see a microphone. To myself, I smiled. I was used to nothing more than a single bored reporter, yawning as he scribbled in a dog-eared notebook.

By tacit consent the TV reporter had the first crack at me. Waving the small directional mike closer to my face, he asked, "Is it true, Lieutenant Hastings, that you captured the suspect in the assassination attempt single-handed?"

"No, that's *not* true. There were three of us inside the building, and probably fifty men outside."

"Why were there only three of you inside, Lieutenant?"

"It was very crowded—very cramped quarters. In a situation like that, too many men can be worse than too few."

"But it was you that actually took him—actually struck the, ah, decisive blow."

"Yes," I answered shortly. "However, I—"

"Were you assigned to guard the governor, Lieutenant?"

As I considered the question, I saw Markham emerging from the elevator. Seeing me, he stood holding the elevator's door open.

Frowning, he raised his chin toward the ceiling. I was wanted upstairs. I was conscious of a small flicker of irritation. Sergeants didn't frown at lieutenants.

"I was going out on another case," I answered automatically. "We were already rolling, in fact, when we got the call about the assassination attempt. Since I was close to the Civic Center, Lieutenant Friedman asked me to take field command. But"—I began to push my way free—"but I'm afraid I'll have to go. Excuse me." As I said it, I glanced apologetically at the camera, as if I were asking its permission to leave.

Markham left me in the hallway outside the police chief's conference room. As a uniformed patrolman opened the door for me, I saw Markham turning toward the trailing gaggle of reporters. Markham was smiling now, anticipating their questions.

Inside the richly furnished conference room, many of the men were already standing. The meeting was breaking up.

"Ah, here he is." Chief Reynolds turned toward me with hand outstretched. "Good work, Lieutenant. *Fine* work." His deep, resonant voice rumbled with good fellowship. The lines around the chief's eyes were personably crinkled.

"Thank you, sir." I allowed him a small victory in our brief handshaking contest.

His expression became unctuous. "The governor," he said solemnly, "will live. The bullet passed through his upper lung. No problem. Barring complications, he could be back to work in a month or so."

"Good."

That duty discharged, he clapped me lightly on the shoulder as he turned me toward the others. "You know everyone, I think."

I looked around the circle, nodding in turn to the district attorney; two assistant D.A.'s; the U.S. attorney; the FBI's local bureau chief; Captain Kreiger, my superior officer; and Friedman. All of them greeted me with murmured congratulations. Then I saw Canelli, still seated. Canelli's face was sweat-sheened. His dark eyes were sheepish. In that company, Canelli wasn't enjoying his role as an essential link in the chain of evidence.

"We're just finishing up," the chief was saying to me, "deciding on jurisdiction and prosecution safeguards and so forth. Captain Kreiger or Lieutenant Friedman can fill you in on the particulars. But we all want you to know how pleased we are that everything went so, ah, smoothly." As he spoke, Reynolds' voice fell to a deeper, more melodious note. I'd always suspected that he practiced his little speeches before a bathroom mirror.

"I'll let Friedman fill him in," Kreiger countered. "I promised to meet with some reporters." Kreiger's squared-off face was stolidly resigned. As captain of Homicide, he'd gone as far up the chain of command as he cared to go. So to Kreiger, the press represented a problem, not a promise.

The meeting broke up quickly, each of the dignitaries collecting a cluster of aides and hangers-on as he bustled toward a waiting elevator. As Friedman and I waited for another elevator, I heard him exhale slowly.

"To think," Friedman said, "that one mentally defective Latino could create all this unseemly scrambling for the spotlight. It's incredible. The governor'll probably end up in the White House, with all this publicity going for him. The mayor will run for governor, naturally. And Chief Reynolds will be mayor. All courtesy of Carlos Ramirez." He pushed me into the empty elevator and punched the fourth-floor button. As we rode down in silence, I was remembering the feel of the shotgun butt as it crashed into the suspect's skull.

"How's Ramirez?" I asked.

Friedman unlocked his office door and gestured me to a chair inside. "He's got a concussion, but no skull fracture. He'll probably be all right."

"How about his mother?"

Friedman shook his head as he lowered himself gratefully into his outsize swivel chair. "She's suffering from muscle spasms of the lower back, shock and heart palpitations. In other words, she isn't so good. And, in fact, his mother's problems seem to have been on Ramirez' mind. He is all steamed up because his mother couldn't get either help for her aching back or welfare. So naturally Ramirez decided to go out and shoot the governor." Friedman paused thoughtfully, then said, "Come to think about it, there's a certain rough justice in all this. His Honor was attacking welfare malingerers. And Ramirez, apparently, was making it a dialogue."

"Have you seen Ramirez yet?"

"No." Friedman sighed ruefully. "I've had my hands full, believe me, just talking to all the reporters and all the publicity-hungry, vote-grabbing politicians, by which term I mean to include Chief Reynolds. Not Kreiger. But Reynolds." Friedman turned to study me reflectively. "You know," he said slowly, "this little exploit of yours could mean a lot to your career. You know that, don't you? Today you're a bona-fide hero, with all the benefits of full TV coverage. *Nationwide* TV coverage, even. It's an ambitious cop's dream of a lifetime."

I decided to shrug.

Friedman held my eye for a last long, speculative moment. Then he also shrugged, at the same time taking a cigar from his desk drawer.

"Those FBI guys," he said, "could give everyone lessons on the gentle art of finessing publicity for themselves. Do you know what that meeting was about—*really* about?"

"I imagine that the FBI's claiming the governor's civil rights were violated."

"Very good, Lieutenant." Friedman nodded deeply. "Literally, they want to make it a federal case. And the mayor and the D.A. and Chief Reynolds, if they went along with the gag, could save the city of San Francisco a bundle in court costs alone. But, naturally, Mister Mayor won't go along with any—"

His phone rang. As Friedman lifted the receiver, he applied a match to his cigar. He listened briefly, then gestured me to the phone as he puffed diligently on the cigar.

"This is Culligan, Lieutenant Hastings. Am I disturbing you?"

"No, it's all right. What've you got?"

"Well, Judy Blake—the girl upstairs from Diane Farley—she had some information, and I thought I should get it to you."

"Fine." I reached for a scratch pad. Friedman supplied a pencil.

"First off," Culligan said, "she thought she recognized the Polaroid shot of the victim. She couldn't give me a name, but she thinks she's seen him around—that is, hanging around Diane Farley's apartment during the past six months. So—" Culligan paused for breath, then continued in his dry, laconic voice. "So after I got her talking a little bit, it develops that this Judy's seen *lots* of men hanging around. So it'll probably turn out that Farley's some kind of a free-lance hooker, or something. And if that's true, then this Judy Blake might've supplied a name for Farley's pimp. She said that—"

"Wait a minute," I interrupted. "Let's finish with the victim. If we assume that Farley is a hooker—a call girl, probably—then the victim was a regular customer. Is that it?"

"Well," Culligan said cautiously, "that's what Judy Blake said. And she seems pretty sharp. But we haven't been able to turn up a corroborating witness."

I checked the time. "It's almost five. Pretty soon, people'll be coming home from work."

"Yeah." Typically, Culligan's voice registered no enthusiasm.

"So is that all you've got on the victim?"

"Well," Culligan hesitated. "When I pressed Judy Blake a little —she's real cagey about committing herself—it turns out that she thinks she saw the victim driving a white Mercedes sports car. A 280SL, she said. And it was parked outside Farley's apartment last night."

"Is she sure about the make and model?"

"Yeah. Her stepfather has one just like it, she says."

"That could be a break. Those cars cost ten or twelve thousand dollars. There probably aren't twenty in the whole city. Is the car missing now?"

"Yeah."

"Maybe the murderer's driving it," I said thoughtfully.

"Yeah."

"Okay. I'll get right on it. Now, what about the pimp?"

"That could be a break, too. Still according to Judy Blake, the name is Jack Winship. Caucasian. Age, approximately twenty-seven. Weight, about a hundred eighty. Height, six foot. Dress, hippie style, but not real far-out. You know—faded jeans and run-down boots and torn sweat shirts. He has scraggly, dirty dark hair that just about touches his shoulders. He wears a long mustache but no beard, although he usually needs a shave. And he wears glasses—heavy black-rimmed glasses."

As I wrote, I said, "Judy Blake sounds like the world's best informant."

"Let's hope." Culligan sighed morosely. I could visualize his long, lantern-jawed face with its chronic smudges of fatigue in the hollows of his eyes. "This Winship drives a beat-up green VW van, with some rust spots and a small stovepipe sticking out of the roof," Culligan continued. "So he shouldn't be too hard to find."

"I'll put him on the air right now. Does Winship actually live with Diane Farley?"

"He comes and goes, apparently. Miss Blake says that if Diane's 'entertaining,' Winship sleeps in his van. But, anyhow, he's always around."

"R and I might just have something on Winship."

"Let's hope," Culligan said again.

"Anything else?"

"Yeah. I aked Judy Blake whether she saw any one of the three —Farley, Winship or the victim—last night. And it turns out that she did. She was home all night studying. And luckily she's got her desk right under the window, so that she can look down into the street. And she's almost sure that she saw Diane Farley and Jack Winship leaving in Winship's van at about six P.M. Judy Blake says that maybe they were going to dinner, which they do a lot, she says—go out to dinner, I mean. So then—" Once more he paused for breath. "So then, about nine thirty, Miss Blake sees the victim pulling up in his white Mercedes."

"Is she sure?"

"She's sure, all right. She won't admit it, but she's sure. She just doesn't quite want to commit herself until she's checked with her father, who's a big shot down in Los Angeles. But, if we needed to, we could pin her down."

"Did she see the victim enter the Farley premises?"

"She didn't actually *eyeball* him, because of the angle of the building. I mean, she couldn't see the door. But she remembers seeing the Mercedes when she went to bed. That was about ten."

"It sounds like the victim had a key to Diane Farley's place."

"That's what I was thinking. Either that, or the door was open."

"I hope you can turn up a few more witnesses like Judy Blake."

"Yeah."

"All right. I'll get things started at this end. You and Sigler keep digging."

"Yessir."

I gave Communications the Winship A.P.B., then buzzed the squad room.

"Is Sergeant Markham around?"

"Nosir. He's—oh, wait. He's talking to a reporter. Shall I get him?"

"Yes." As I said it, I was aware of a small tic of jealousy as I thought of Markham charming the reporters with his lean, hard-eyed good looks. I fidgeted irritably through a full half-minute before Markham came on the line. I ordered him to get a list of all registered owners of Mercedes 280SL sports cars in the Bay Area, then begin checking them out against the drivers' licenses of the registered owners, comparing physical characteristics with those of the victim. Additionally, I wanted Communications advised of the possibility that Farley and Winship could be traveling together, either in the VW van or the Mercedes. And, finally, I wanted the day's Missing Persons reports checked against the list of 280SL owners. Remembering the half-minute delay, I issued the orders cryptically. Markham's acknowledgment was equally cryptic.

As I hung up, I saw Friedman eying me with obvious amusement.

"One of these days," he pronounced, "Markham could be giving you orders. Do you realize that? You. Not me."

"Why not you?"

"Because by that time—when Kreiger retires—I'll be retired, too. You will then be the logical choice for captain—provided that in the meantime you've learned enough to bestow a few judicious kisses on a few carefully selected asses. Otherwise, like I say, Markham will surely be the boss. Already, he's jockeying for position—which is to say that he's already beginning to probe for your weakness. Yours. Not mine."

"Why not yours?"

"Because he knows you're his problem—his antagonist. Both of you are big-bull-moose types, pawing the ground. Kreiger, too. But I'm just a"—Friedman spread his hands—"I'm just an overweight ex-actor. That's the trouble with once having acted: you never quite get a fresh grip on reality. However, I'm smart, so I get by. Whereas, like I said, you're an instinctive stud—a heavy. But you spend a lot of energy repressing the instinct. Because, really, you don't enjoy leaning on people. Markham, of course, has no such hangups. He—"

The phone rang. Friedman puffed leisurely at his cigar through two more rings, then answered. He listened for a full minute without speaking, then hung up. He looked at the phone for a moment, then smiled inscrutably. "That was the chief," he said. "He told me to tell you that you're to hold yourself in readiness for a special assignment."

"What is it?"

"Well, it seems that some network execs got together over a few martinis, or something, and decided that they're going to do an in-depth program on the assassination attempt. They're going to give it the 'Violence in America' angle. It sounds like a socko cast, with a little something for everyone. They're going to have the governor's wife, for the fan-mag types, and a psychologist for the intellectuals, and you for the cops-and-robbers fans. And, of course, they'll have the chief, so that everyone'll know we've got a chief who looks like a chief should look."

"Not you."

"No. Not me. I don't look the part, unlike you and the chief. So I guess I'll go home." He got his gun out of the drawer, clipped it on, and pushed himself to his feet, grunting with the effort. "Good luck with the Diane Farley case," he said casually, taking his hat from a filing cabinet. "It sounds like it might have a few interesting kinks. And good luck with the governor's wife. Don't let her upstage you. I understand she's good at that. And whatever you do, keep your best side to the camera."

Eight

"Jesus," Canelli breathed, "this is just like Hollywood, or something. Look at those lights. It looks like a different squad room."

"Maybe I can get you a speaking part, Canelli. Interested?"

He looked at me quickly. Seeing my smile, he smiled in return. Then he frowned. Had the publicity bug bitten Canelli, too? I couldn't be sure.

"She's certainly pretty," he whispered, nodding toward the governor's wife. "She's a lot younger than he is, isn't she?"

"She's his second wife. At least." I watched her arranging herself beside Chief Reynolds. She moved with the deft assurance of a model. Ten minutes ago, I'd heard one of the television executives suggesting that she apply some extra shadow around her eyes, "to be sure the idea of tragedy gets across." Now the psychoanalyst was taking his place. At the same time, Chief Reynolds was alternately clearing his throat, smiling tentatively at the camera and adjusting his cuffs. He was wearing a business suit. The mayor had suggested a uniform, but the TV exec had vetoed the idea as being "too militaristic for a national audience." As proof, he'd cited the astronauts: officers in mufti.

The executive gestured to a sizable group of inspectors and uniformed men, lounging on desks and chairs, watching the unprecedented bustle. "Some of you can get in the background."

The executive spoke in a high, nervous voice. With his mod clothes and affected gestures, he seemed strangely out of place directing policemen. "Stand about five feet behind the three principals," he said. "You know, in a loose group. Like you're onlookers." He waved his hands at them, as if to boost them impatiently into place. "All right. Let's have the lights."

As the lights came on, Canelli whispered, "What about you, Lieutenant? I thought you were going to be interviewed, too."

I shrugged. "They're playing it by ear, I guess."

"Maybe you should remind them you're here."

I mimicked his conspirator's hiss. "Give it time, Canelli. I don't even have my makeup on. And besides, I—"

The executive was suddenly turning toward me, biting his lip and frowning. In three quick springy strides, he was beside me. "Listen, Lieutenant," he said, "I just now heard that the network's only clearing us for a five-minute shot, instead of fifteen. It's a hell of a note, with all this equipment. I mean, I wouldn't've gone through all this, just for five minutes. I'd've shot it live, like a news segment, instead of taping it and everything. But, anyhow, the focus is going to be on the governor's wife. Okay?"

"You don't want me, you mean."

"Not for this sequence. I mean, this is taped, like I said. We've got you on local footage, haven't we?"

"Yes."

"Well, good. That's about all we can— *Wait*," he said sharply, gesturing pettishly to the closest camera. "You're duplicating *angles*. Go to your *right*, for God's sake." As he moved away, he looked at me and shrugged, spreading his hands.

"Well," Canelli said, "that's show biz, I guess, Lieutenant. I guess they're—"

Someone touched my arm. Turning, I saw a blond patrolman.

"Communications asked me to find you, Lieutenant Hastings. They'd like you to call them."

I moved to the far corner of the squad room, stepping over a tangle of electrical cables.

I spoke softly into the phone: "This is Lieutenant Hastings."

"This is Blanchard in Communications, Lieutenant."

"Yes, what is it, Blanchard?"

"On that Diane Farley A.P.B., they've picked her up."

"Where?"

"Santa Barbara."

"Do you have any particulars?"

"No, but a Detective Woolsey is standing by in Santa Barbara. I have a phone number for him."

"All right. Get him, and put the call through to my office. I'll be there in two minutes." I gestured to Canelli, who was dividing his attention between me and the cameras. I told him where I was going, and ordered him to bring Markham to my office as soon as possible.

As I was switching on my office lights, the phone rang.

"I have Sergeant Woolsey for you, Lieutenant," Blanchard said.

"Good. Put him on." I sat behind my desk, moving a notepad and ball-point pen closer to hand. After the routine pleasantries, I asked Woolsey for the particulars.

He replied in a soft southern drawl: "We picked her up about five miles north of Santa Barbara, at approximately five forty-five P.M. Just a little more than an hour ago. We're holding her on a vag charge and suspicion of Grand Theft Auto."

"What kind of a car was she driving?"

"The one described in your supplemental: a white Mercedes 280SL, license number CVC 916. Registered to one Thomas King, 2267 Vallejo Street, San Francisco."

As I copied down the information, I asked, "What kind of documentation have you got, Sergeant?"

"We've got the car registration and the license plate, both of which checked out with DMV, cross-checking the engine number. Then we've got a billfold, I.D., driver's license and credit cards, all made out to Thomas King. They were in the glove compartment."

"Do you have his driver's license right there?"

"Right in front of me, Lieutenant. I figured you'd be asking."

"Give me a description of Thomas King, then."

"Well," Woolsey drawled, "he's—lessee—he's forty-three years old, five ten, weighs a hundred seventy-five. Brown eyes, brown hair. Looking at his picture, I'd say he's a kind of a smooth-looking guy. Down here, we'd call him actorish. Then there's the car, of course. It costs ten thousand, so they tell me."

"At least." As I said it, Canelli and Markham came into the office. I covered the phone, whispering, "Diane Farley's in custody. And we've got an I.D. on the victim."

Canelli whistled softly. Markham merely nodded, as if he'd expected the news. His lean, handsome face was impassive.

"What about the girl?" I asked Woolsey. "Does she have any I.D.?"

"Negative. But she says her name is Diane Farley."

"What's her story?"

"She says she borrowed the car from a friend. Thomas King, that is. It's not a very original story, of course. But she's doing the best she can with it."

"What's her frame of mind? How's she acting?"

"Pretty cool," Woolsey said after a moment's pause. "Pretty cool indeed. According to her, she just took a little old ride down to San Diego last night, and then decided to go back to San Francisco today."

I frowned. "What'd you mean, go back?"

"I mean that she was traveling north on 101 when we picked her up," Woolsey answered. "And we found a San Diego gas receipt. So offhand I'd say her story checks out. Of course, with your want out on her, we never did figure to do more than hold her, so we haven't asked her any real hard questions."

"Yes, that's right," I answered absently. "By the way, did you give her her rights?"

"We sure did, Lieutenant. First thing we got her out of the car. No problem there."

60

"Good. I'll send three men down there—two for the subject, one for the car. Unless—" I hesitated.

On cue, Woolsey said, "If it'll help out you boys, I could get one of my men, and we could bring them *both* up there. The girl and the car, I mean. I wouldn't mind seeing how that little old car runs."

I smiled. "All right. Fine. Can you leave tonight?"

"Sure thing, Lieutenant. Matter of fact, we're all ready to go. No sweat."

"You could probably have her here by, say, ten o'clock tomorrow morning, then."

"As good as done, Lieutenant. As good as done."

"I'll see you tomorrow, then. Ask for me. At the Hall of Justice."

"Roger."

I handed Markham the slip of notepaper. "That's probably the victim's name and address. But you'd better get a copy of his picture. Check him out." I turned to Canelli. "You go, too. Let's figure on meeting here at nine o'clock tomorrow morning, to see what we've got."

As my office door closed behind them, I sagged back in my chair, closing my eyes. I hadn't eaten since lunch—since the leisurely bantering hour I'd spent with Friedman.

Had we really talked so lightly about Friedman's past and present—and about the governor's political scheming? And, an hour later, had I really crashed the wooden stock of a shotgun against the bone of a boy's skull? Had I then driven to Hoffman Street, where I'd stared into the lusterless brown eyes of a corpse? All in six short hours?

I opened my eyes slowly, and checked the time. It was almost eight. All day long, I hadn't called Ann.

Wearily, I picked up the phone. After three rings, I heard her voice on the line.

"It's me, Ann."

"Oh—" She seemed startled. Then, in a low, guarded voice: "Hello, Frank."

Not "darling." Not a single soft "hello," meant just for me.

"What's wrong?" I asked.

I heard her sigh before she said, "Nothing. My—the boys' father is here."

"Oh." I allowed a moment of silence to pass before I said, "I was going to stop by for a few minutes."

"Yes. Please."

"You're sure it's all right? Will he be gone?"

"Maybe."

"But you don't care."

"No."

"All right. I'll see you in twenty minutes."

"Frank?"

"Yes?"

"Are you all right?"

"I'm tired, that's all. I'll see you soon."

She whispered, "Goodbye, darling."

Nine

As I switched off the engine and set the parking brake, I was thinking of the first time I'd come to the Haywood flat, just three months ago. It had been a business call. Dan Haywood, Ann's teen-age son, had briefly been a suspect in a homicide. I'd been questioning Dan on the front porch when I'd heard someone behind me. Turning, I'd seen a small, stylish blonde standing in the rain, holding two large, sodden grocery bags. With my cop's compulsion for quick categorization, I'd labeled Ann a young society matron— cool, self-confident, aloof. I'd been right about the past, but not about the present. She'd been married to a successful, affluent psychoanalyst. But the marriage had ended two years ago. Now she lived with her two sons and taught grammar school to supplement her child-support allotment. I'd only met her husband once. It had been a brief, blustering encounter. If I continued to threaten his son, my career would be in jeopardy, he'd said. The threats had been routine. The delivery, though, had been convincing. Victor Haywood was a vicious, pompous, polysyllabic sadist. During most of their marriage, his secret victim had been his wife. She was only now, two years later, rediscovering a sense of her own worth.

As I walked to Ann's front door, I saw a Porsche parked two doors down. Dr. Haywood drove nothing but sports cars.

Billy, age eleven, answered the door. "Hey," he said in his high, excited voice. "Hey. Jeeze. You were on TV. Jeeze, they talked more about you than the governor, practically."

"Not true, Billy. Besides, by tomorrow, I'll be yesterday's news."

"How many times did you shoot the crook? How many?"

I sighed. "If you'd listened, Billy, you'd know that I didn't shoot him at all."

"He was shooting at you, though. I *know* he was shooting at you. I *heard* about that."

Ann came up behind the boy, grasped his shoulders firmly, and turned him back toward the living room. "Hi," she said softly, squeezing my hand. "Come in." As we walked side by side down the short hallway of the converted Victorian flat, she moved close beside me. As our thighs brushed, I felt a sudden, secret quickening of desire. Again she squeezed my hand. She felt it, too.

Dan was seated beside his father on the sofa. Seeing me, Dan smiled. "Hi, Frank. You're a big hero today. Great."

"Today is right. I was just telling Billy that, in the news business, it's all today."

"Hello, Lieutenant." Pointedly, Victor Haywood didn't bother to look at me directly.

"Hello, Doctor. How've you been?"

"Fine, Lieutenant. Just fine. How've *you* been?" His eyes were mocking, his voice elaborately supercilious. He was a lean, taut man with a cruel mouth and a permanent country-club tan. In that moment I suddenly realized that he would always hate me— first for threatening his son with the law, then for becoming his ex-wife's lover.

"How do you manage to get such a good press for yourself, Lieutenant?" he was asking. "Do you trade favors? Is that how it's done?"

Staring directly into his saturnine eyes, I deliberately allowed a long moment of silence to elapse before I quietly said, "No, Doctor, that's not how it's done."

"Oh, come on now, Lieutenant. I've always heard that policemen can get the law at a wholesale price, so to speak—just like car salesmen can get cars at cost. Surely you can work a swap with a friendly reporter. Cut-rate cars or cut-rate laws. What's the difference? Everyone's looking for a deal."

"Not everyone. Not me."

"In that case, Lieutenant, I submit that you're naïve—or worse."

"And I submit that you're wrong—or worse."

As we held each other's eyes, I saw his fixed, malevolent smile falter. I realized that I was playing a dangerous game, ridiculing an egotist before his sons. If I could, I decided to go for a draw.

His voice was low and tight. "One of us, obviously, is wrong. Very, very wrong. The question is, which one?"

In the silence, I heard Ann clear her throat. Dan was staring down at the floor. Billy's eyes were wide as he looked first at me, then at his father.

It seemed to require an enormous effort, but I shrugged. "Lots of people have misconceptions about policemen—just like lots of people have misconceptions about psychiatrists."

He nodded, mocked thoughtfully. "Very neatly put, Lieutenant. I keep forgetting that you once went to college."

I didn't reply. Instead, without being invited, I sat down in a large leather armchair. It was a chair that had once been the doctor's favorite. Victor Haywood watched me for a moment, then rose to his feet. He turned to Ann, who had also risen to face her ex-husband. I saw her hands clenched knuckle-white. She couldn't hold her own with Haywood. She just couldn't hit hard enough.

"I want you to be sure and remember, now," Haywood said, "that the boys are to be ready, without fail, at four P.M. Friday. I'll be here precisely at four to pick them up, and I intend to be underway by four thirty at the latest. Otherwise, the whole weekend will be jeopardized. Skiing takes an enormous amount of energy, you know, even without the strain of adjusting to the altitude. So it's essential that the boys get a good night's sleep Friday night. Especially Billy. He doesn't tolerate altitude changes well."

"I know," Ann answered. Her voice was low. Her eyes fell.

"Yes. Well, knowing is one thing. Taking measures is something else."

"They'll be ready, Victor. We'll pack Thursday night."

"Yes. However, don't pack *too* much. Don't overdo it. Remember, it'll be three of us in a sports car."

She didn't reply.

Abruptly, Haywood turned to his two sons, sitting on the opposite arms of the couch. Their farewells were perfunctory. Haywood left the flat without glancing at me.

"Well," Dan said, "it's almost eight. I'd better hit the books. See you, Frank."

I rose. "See you, Dan."

Reluctantly, Billy followed his older brother down the hallway to the rear of the house. Ann stood in the doorway, watching them go. When the hallway door closed I went to her, turned her around, and took her in my arms. I felt her tremble.

"He's a genuine twenty-four-carat bastard," I said, tucking her head down in the hollow of my shoulder. "I think he's the biggest stuffed shirt I've ever known."

Her voice was muffled. "Thank you for giving it back to him, darling. Most people don't, you know—or can't. He intimidates most people."

"I suppose he does. In a way, that's his trade." I drew her closer. I could feel her body slowly relaxing against mine. "But it just so happens that it's my trade, too," I said softly.

She drew back to look at me. Her eyes were misted with a hint of tears, but her smile was bright. Disengaging one hand, she pressed at the tip of my nose with a small, slim forefinger.

"You don't intimidate me, Lieutenant," she whispered. "You're nothing but a sentimental slob. And don't you forget it."

Ten

"Well," Friedman said, sinking into my visitor's chair, "I understand your last night's performance was left on the cutting-room
floor. Obviously, you ignored my advice concerning the governor's lady. You got upstaged."

"It didn't even get as far as the cutting room."

"Still, your local coverage was good. Excellent, in fact. When
are our three underlings due?"

"Nine o'clock."

He checked the time. "They have four minutes. You want some
coffee?"

"No, thanks." I was absently riffling through my copies of yesterday's homicide interrogations. Most of them were dead, concerned with cases that would never be solved.

"How many've you got?" Friedman asked, pointing to the
interrogation reports.

"Sixteen. How about you?"

"Fourteen," he answered complacently. "As they say, seniority
has its privileges. Have we got anything more on the King thing?"

"I don't know. I left last night without talking to Culligan. But
he was still working on it, I know—checking out Farley's neighbors."

"If Culligan was still working, there'll be new information. He's a bulldog. A gaunt, cadaverous bulldog. And he's especially good at conducting investigations after dark. Do you know why?"

"Why?"

"Because if he has to work at night, he doesn't have to be with his wife, who also happens to be cadaverous. Have you ever met her? She's—"

A knock sounded on my office door, followed by all three men: Markham, Canelli and Culligan. I motioned them to chairs and tore off the top page of my scratch pad. The page was covered by doodles, one of which was "Ann" printed in big block letters. As I crumpled it up, I caught Friedman's knowing leer.

"Let's start with you, Culligan," I said brusquely. "What've you got?"

Culligan opened his notebook on the desk and sighed heavily over the meticulously written pages. Typically, his manner seemed to presage an admission of defeat. But just as typically, he'd discovered something of potential value.

"Sigler and I did quite a bit of digging," Culligan began. "And, first thing, we pretty much corroborated everything that Judy Blake said." He glanced directly at me. "It's like I figured—she's a good witness."

I nodded.

"Also," Culligan continued, "we turned up something else. We got two different witnesses who said that they saw a black guy leaving Diane Farley's apartment sometime around ten thirty Tuesday night. And we also have testimony that the victim was probably still inside the apartment at the time. Or at least his car was still parked outside."

"What *kind* of a black guy?" Friedman asked.

Culligan glanced at his notes, then looked apologetically at Friedman. "We didn't get much of a description. I mean, it was dark, and"—Culligan waved his hand—"and you know how it is, especially if the informant's Caucasian."

"Did the subject get into a car?" I asked.

"I don't think so."

"How'd this black guy seem?" Markham asked. "Was he acting suspiciously?"

Culligan spread his hands, at the same time rolling his tongue inside his mouth, as if he were reacting to something sour. "One witness said he was acting suspiciously, one said he wasn't. Me, I'd rather not guess."

"This black guy could've been one of Farley's clients," Friedman offered, "not the murderer. After all, the facts are that Thomas King was murdered in Farley's apartment, and Farley was caught driving King's car. That's a pretty potent set of circumstances. The way it looks now, either Farley or Winship—or both —are our best suspects. We don't want to jump to any conclusions, just because someone saw a black guy wandering around."

Culligan decided not to comment.

"What else did you find out?" I asked.

"Not much, Lieutenant. At least, not much that's new. No one saw Diane Farley come home. No one saw Jack Winship and his van after six P.M. No one heard anything suspicious. We *did* get considerable confirmation of Judy Blake's statement that Diane Farley had lots of men running in and out, but whether she was actually in business as a hooker still isn't clear. At least, it's not clear to me. A couple that lives in the same building—in the other apartment on the ground floor—told me that Farley was a model."

Markham snorted. "Every hooker I've ever collared said she was a model."

"This one had the pictures to prove it, though," I said.

Markham shrugged with slow, deliberate insolence. Looking into mine, his gray eyes were expressionless.

As I returned his stare, I asked him, "What about the victim? How's he check out?"

Taking his notebook from his pocket, Markham continued our eye-locked contest. Then, coolly, he lowered his eyes to his notes. No decision. No winner, no loser. "Thomas King," he said. "Age forty-three. Address, 2267 Vallejo—which is a good address. Occupation, film maker."

"Ah, so," Friedman said. "The victim is a film maker, the suspect is a model. What'll you bet Thomas King made dirty movies?"

Markham shook his head. "Not if you believe his wife. He made documentaries and advertising commercials. Naturally, I'll check him out today—business associations, bank balance, reputation. But I'd bet that he's clean."

"No one's clean," Friedman said. "In this business, that's the first rule. Everyone's dirty, even if it's just the tiniest little smudge."

Markham didn't respond.

"What else?" I asked. "What about his family?"

Again Markham consulted his notes. "The wife's name is Marjorie, age forty. They have a son named Bruce, seventeen years old. The wife works as the manager of an antique business. The son is a senior at Lowell High School."

"How'd the wife react to the news of her husband's death?" Friedman asked.

Markham thought about it. "She seemed pretty cool. She seemed to be mostly concerned about how her son would react. Her son was out when I got there."

"Did she report her husband missing?"

"Yes. But not until nine A.M. yesterday morning—Wednesday."

Friedman thoughtfully regarded the tip of his cigar. "As you say, she's pretty cool. Most women call by one or two in the morning."

"She claims she's a sound sleeper. She knew her husband was going to be out. So she went to sleep and didn't wake up until morning. They have twin beds."

Friedman shook his head. "I don't buy it. Women just don't operate like that."

"If you talked to her," Markham answered, "you might change your mind. She . . ." He hesitated. "She comes on pretty strong."

"Where did her husband say he was going Tuesday night?" I asked.

"She said it was business. He did a lot of night work down at his studio, apparently. Two, three times a week, he didn't come home. It's taken for granted."

"What did Mrs. King say when you told her how and where her husband was murdered?"

"She didn't say much—didn't commit herself. And of course I soft-pedaled the idea that there might be a sex angle."

Friedman nodded approval. "Very wise. Cops can get sued, you know. And do."

A moment of thoughtful silence descended as each man looked off in a different direction. Obviously, there was no more information to exchange. Finally Friedman heaved a sigh, signifying the end of the meeting. He looked at me, saying, "Why don't we have Markham check out Thomas King's background, and have Culligan check out this black guy, if possible? When she arrives, you and Canelli can grill Diane Farley while I, ah, coordinate things. Plus, I've got a meeting with a couple of assistant D.A.'s on the Ramirez thing."

"How's Ramirez doing?" I asked.

"I haven't checked yet this morning."

As the three inspectors left the office, my phone rang. "This is Olsen, Lieutenant. In the crime lab. I've got a report for you on the knife found at the scene of the Hoffman Street homicide. Do you want it verbally, or should I send the report up to you?"

"Both."

"Oh. Well—" Olsen cleared his throat. "Well, first, we found that the blood on the weapon matched the John Doe's blood type.

"His name is King. Thomas King."

"Oh. Thanks. I'll just make a note of that on the report." During the brief silence, I could visualize Olsen carefully erasing "John Doe" and inscribing "Thomas King." Olsen was a meticulous man. Finally he was ready to continue. "We also lifted two partial fingerprints, and one that was almost intact. We're sending them off to Sacramento and Washington."

"Good."

"Those were the two main things we found," Olsen said. "However, inside the knife, we found a couple of things that might help you. Besides, that is, just pocket lint."

"What things?"

"First, we found a few grains of marijuana."

"Oh."

"And then we found tracings of magnesium and aluminum oxide."

I wrote down the two terms. "What's with the magnesium and aluminum oxide?" I asked. "Any ideas?"

"Well, sir, we've talked about it down here, and we came up with three main possibilities—either firecrackers or flares, or maybe fire bombs. Magnesium, you know, is used for all three. Mostly, I guess, for flares. If you don't count military-type fire bombs. But aluminum oxide, although it burns, I'd say mostly it'd be used for firecrackers—for the colors, you know, when they burn."

As I thoughtfully doodled "flares," "firecrackers" and "bombs," my other phone rang. Friedman took the call, and we both hung up at the same time. "That was the desk," he said. "Sergeant what's-his-name from Santa Barbara is in the squad room with Diane Farley."

Eleven

"Sit down, Miss Farley." I faced her across a small metal table. On the table was an ashtray, a microphone and a salmon-colored file folder: Diane Farley's "jacket." There was only one item on her rap sheet. Fourteen months ago, on the complaint of one Lester Gaines, Diane Farley and an alleged male accomplice had been arrested on an extortion charge. The accomplice had been tried and acquitted. The charge against Diane Farley had been changed to suspicion of soliciting for immoral purposes, then dropped for lack of evidence.

Canelli closed the door and moved to his accustomed position, standing to the subject's right, leaning against the wall of the small, windowless interrogation room. According to departmental regulations, both Canelli and I had checked our revolvers with the hallway guard outside.

Without speaking, I sat for a full minute watching Diane Farley squirm. I assessed her carefully, feature by feature, line by line, twitch by twitch. She seemed slimmer than her pictures, almost skinny. Her mouse-colored hair fell to her shoulders in dirty tangles. Her complexion was sallow and blotched. She wore a nondescript sweater, corduroy slacks and expensive-looking laced boots. In her eyes I could plainly see the characteristic muddy, sullen dullness of defeat that marks those who live on the far side of the law.

She sat round-shouldered in her chair, exhausted. She looked defeated, ready to cave in. Yet I knew, instinctively, that Diane Farley would be tough.

I pointed to the microphone. "Do you have any objection to our recording this interrogation, Miss Farley?"

She looked at the microphone. I saw her frown.

"Yeah, I mind." Her voice was harsh, roughened by both defiance and fatigue. "I mind this whole thing. What the hell *is* all this, anyhow?"

I moved the microphone aside. Speaking quietly, I verified that she'd received her rights on two different occasions: first when she was apprehended in Santa Barbara, next when she was booked by us on suspicion of Grand Theft Auto, less than an hour ago. Acknowledging that she'd received her rights, she spoke in surly monosyllables. Her eyes moved restlessly, flicking around the room, then darting to Canelli and myself before falling finally to the small metal table.

"Would you like to smoke, Miss Farley?"

She shook her head.

I fingered an appendix to her booking form. It was a request for the court to appoint a lawyer.

"You don't have a lawyer of your own?"

Again she shook her head. She began to pick at the edge of the table with a broken, dirty thumbnail.

"How old are you, Miss Farley?"

She drew a long, slow breath. "Twenty-four."

"How long have you lived in San Francisco?"

"Three years."

"How long have you lived at 436 Hoffman?"

"Six, seven months. I forget."

"Where did you live before you came to San Francisco?"

"I lived in Chicago."

"Were you ever arrested in Chicago?"

Her glance glittered with quick malevolence. "I never had any trouble with the law in my whole life until I came here."

74

"Have you ever lived anywhere but San Francisco and Chicago?"

"No. And I wish I'd stayed in Chicago, too."

"How long have you known Thomas King, Miss Farley?"

For a moment she didn't reply. Her face was averted. As she continued to pick at the table edge, her thumb was whitening with strain. "What about that lawyer? What the hell happened to my lawyer, anyhow?"

"The court will appoint one. That's a legal matter. It's got nothing to do with us."

"Then I don't have to answer. Not without a lawyer."

"That's right, you don't," I said readily. "However, if you've got nothing to hide from us, there's no point in not answering my last question. It's a simple request for information. I want to find out how long you knew Thomas King. I could ask the same question of his wife."

"That's assuming I know him."

I nodded. "That's true, Miss Farley. That's the assumption I'm making—that you knew Thomas King. Am I wrong?"

The muscles in her neck were corded now. She was swallowing rapidly. The fingers of her left hand, flat on the table, were beginning to tremble. Quickly she snatched the hand into her lap. Her voice was a ragged whisper. "No, you're not wrong. I knew him."

I decided to ease her along slowly, past the point where a lawyer could help her. I'd mix up my questions, pretending a friendly concern. Then I'd begin applying pressure. "How long have you known him?" I pitched my voice to a low, confidential note.

"Ab—" She swallowed. "About six months, I guess. Maybe longer."

"You said you've lived at 436 Hoffman for six or seven months. Did you know Thomas King before you moved to your present address?"

"For a little while. Not long."

"Where did you live before, Miss Farley?"

"Before when?"

"Before you moved to Hoffman Street."

Her sidelong glance was furtive. "I, ah, lived different places. I moved a lot."

"You didn't have any permanent address?"

She shrugged, then nodded.

"You lived with men." It was a casual, offhand statement—not a question.

Again she shrugged, then said, "Maybe I'll have a cigarette after all. I mean, I don't really smoke. But . . ." She let it go unfinished. Canelli gave her a cigarette and held a match for her. She inhaled deeply, then blew out a ragged, tremulous smoke-plume.

Silently I watched her smoke half the cigarette. She smoked ravenously, drawing the smoke into her lungs in short, sharp gasps. She kept her eyes averted. I gestured to the file folder, lying closed on the table. "I'm not trying to hang you for a few tricks you've turned, Diane," I said quietly. "This isn't a vice roust. It's not *any* kind of a roust. I'm just interested in the death of Thomas King. Do you understand?"

She snorted. "I understand what you're saying. But I don't have to believe you."

"No, you don't. But you'd be a fool *not* to believe me." I gestured again to the folder. "That's your file—your jacket, we call it. I know all about the beef you had fourteen months ago. But that beef's got nothing to do with me—with this investigation. Not unless you're uncooperative."

"What's *that* supposed to mean?" She savagely twisted out her cigarette.

I sighed. "It's supposed to mean that if you'll go along with me, I'll go along with you. We can do it the easy way or the hard way."

"Well, what's so important about me—about where I lived before, and everything?"

"I like to know who I'm talking to, Miss Farley. It's as simple as that. For instance, I'd like to know why you decided to get your own place, after just—living around."

Long Way Down

I'd struck an unsuspected nerve.

"I decided to get my own place," she flared, "because I got tired of—of getting thrown out on my ass, every time I didn't feel like doing tricks in bed. It—it's as simple as that. It—" She stared balefully down at the jacket, her mouth working. Finally, in a low, harsh whisper, she said, "It's not always like it says in your goddamn reports, you know. I mean, just because you write it down and then get some poor bastard to sign it, that don't"—she suddenly gulped—"that don't make it so. That don't make it so at *all.*" Her voice was ragged, close to cracking. She was slumping in her chair, deadly tired. Fatigue was loosening her tongue. Fatigue, and a suddenly overwhelming sense of self-pity.

"We're saying the same thing, Miss Farley." I gestured negligently toward the folder. "I already told you, I'm not interested in what's there. I just want your story."

The twisted curve of her lips shaped a silent obscenity. "My story is really very simple, Lieutenant. Very goddamn simple. I never knew my father, as the saying goes. And my mother, so called, didn't give a goddamn what happened to me, just so long as I stayed out of her bedroom at night. I don't mean that she was a hooker. She wasn't. She just liked men more than she liked me, is all. So I got married when I was seventeen—the same age as my mother always said she got married, except she really didn't. I had that on her, anyhow. I actually got married, but she never did. And I think it maybe bugged her. I really do. So then, the next thing, I got pregnant. So my husband, naturally, took off—just like my father did. Or anyway, the way my mother *said* he did. There's a difference, I find out. There's a big goddamn difference. So then"—she paused, drawing a deep, unsteady breath—"so then I had an abortion. And abortions, you know, don't come cheap. So—" Again she paused. She was frowning, staring fixedly down at the file folder. Her voice had slipped to a lower, more distant note.

"So you took money from men." I spoke very softly—suggesting, not accusing.

77

She nodded slowly. "Right. Like you say, I took money from men. I didn't have any choice. I mean, abortionists don't take IOU's, you know."

"So then you came out here, to San Francisco."

"Yeah," she answered bitterly. "I came out here. And what a mistake *that* was. I mean, I'd always heard that San Francisco was the place to come, especially if you don't mind taking your clothes off once in a while. And, for a while, that's what I did. I mean, I was a go-go girl. But then I found out that it's just another hustle, being a go-go girl. That money, at first, seems pretty good. But you never see any of it. So then—" She raised one hand from the table in a small gesture of exhausted resignation. "So then I moved in with a guy. And then another guy. And, between times, I started modeling for a couple of—you know—photographers."

"I saw some of the pictures." She looked up sharply, surprised. "In your apartment."

Her eyes narrowed. "Yeah. Well, if you saw them, you know that I don't model for any hard-core stuff. I mean, I don't mind taking my clothes off, like I said. There's nothing wrong with that. Especially not now—not in the past few years. But that's it. Period. I mean, I had lots of chances to—you know—pose with men. But I never did. Those pictures you saw in my place, that's it, as far as I'm concerned. Period. No fun and games."

I nodded somberly, pandering to her outraged hooker's virtue. Then, to ease off momentarily, I said, "Your apartment puzzled me."

"Yeah?"

"It looks—" I hesitated. "It looks like it belongs to a hippie, almost. And that doesn't seem to be your bag."

"Yeah. Well, you're right. I rented it furnished, see? I got all that furniture for two hundred dollars. Not that I like it. But I took it." She shrugged. "One of these days I'll move."

"So you've lived there for six months."

She nodded. Her head bobbed loosely. She was surrendering to fatigue.

"And, during the past six months, you've been doing what you did before. Modeling."

Again she nodded loosely.

"And once in a while you—have a man in."

She didn't reply, didn't stir. But she didn't deny it. She was coming around, answering more readily.

"How'd you happen to meet Thomas King? Did you pose for him? Is that how you met him?"

"No. I—" She hesitated, glancing first at me, then at Canelli. It was her final moment of decision. When she finally sighed, one last time, I knew that I had her. "I posed for a friend of Tom's," she said.

I picked up a pencil. "Who was that, Miss Farley?"

"His name is Roger Sobel."

"So you worked for Sobel, and met Thomas King through him."

"Yeah."

"And so King started—coming around."

She smiled bitterly. "Yeah. Right. He started 'coming around' pretty often, as a matter of fact."

"How often?"

She shrugged. "Once a week, maybe."

"Did you ever go out anywhere together? For dinner, or drinks?"

"No. He just—came around."

"Would he phone first?"

"Sometimes."

"Did he phone Tuesday?"

"No."

"What time did King usually arrive at your place?"

"Nine or ten. Sometime in there."

"And how long would he stay?"

She shrugged. "Until one o'clock, maybe. Sometimes later."

"Did he ever stay overnight?"

"Once or twice, when he was supposed to be—you know—out of town. Can I have another cigarette?"

As Canelli stepped quickly forward, lighting her cigarette, I decided to shift my ground. "You and Jack Winship went out about six Tuesday evening. Is that right?"

She looked up sharply, surprised. "Did—did I say anything about Jack?"

I shook my head, staring at her silently. Then: "You and Winship *did* go out about six, though, didn't you?"

She dropped her eyes, frowning down at the cigarette. Finally she nodded. "Yeah, I guess it was about six. Maybe a little later."

"Were you going to eat dinner?"

"Well, we started out to eat dinner. We went down to The Shed."

"Where's that?"

"Down on Twenty-fourth Street. Just ten blocks or so from where I live."

"All right. Then what?"

"Well, we—we started drinking. Wine. There were some people there. Friends of Jack's—people he'd known up in Portland, or somewhere. So we all started drinking, like I said. Then we had something to eat. And then more wine. So finally"—she drew sharply on the cigarette—"so finally it got to be eleven o'clock, and we were all gassed. So I said I wanted to go. And Jack, he didn't want to leave."

"Why?"

She shrugged sullenly. "He just wanted to stay, that's all. And I wanted to leave."

"So what did you do?"

"I started walking. I mean, I told that son of a bitch where he could shove it, and I started walking. Like I said, it's only ten or twelve blocks. It's no big deal."

"What time did you get home?"

"Eleven, I guess. Maybe later. I was—well, I'd been drinking, like I said. And I—"

"Did you expect to find Thomas King at your place?"

"No. I already told you, I—"

"Did you expect to find anyone? Any—friend? Any John?"

"No," she answered plaintively. "I already *told* you. I just—"

"Were you drunk when you arrived home?"

She finished her cigarette and ground out the butt in the ashtray. She began to shake her head in a dull, dogged arc. "I wasn't drunk. Not really drunk. I was—you know—just high, that's all."

"All right. Now, what happened when you got to your place? I want you to tell me exactly what happened."

"Yeah. Well, there—" She licked at her lips. "There isn't much to tell. I mean, I—I just went inside, and I—I found him dead."

"Was the outside door locked when you entered your apartment?"

"Well, I—I suppose so. Yeah."

"Do you always carry a key?"

"Sure I do. I mean, around this city, you'd goddamn better lock your doors. This is the goddamnedest—"

"Did Thomas King have a key, too?"

She sighed. "Yeah, he had one."

"All right. So you went inside. Where was the body?"

"In—in my bedroom. Between the bed and the wall."

"Was he facing the bed or the wall?"

"The—the wall, I think." She nodded, frowning. "Yeah, the wall."

"All right. What happened then?"

"Well, I—Christ, I don't remember. Not really. I mean, about the first thing I remember, I was throwing up."

"Where did you throw up?"

"In the toilet."

"Then what happened?"

"Well, then I—I had to go to the toilet."

"Yes. Then what?"

"Well, then I guess I just—just kind of wandered around. I remember that, first, I didn't think he was dead. I mean, I didn't see how he *could* be dead. Not there. Not in my—my apartment.

So I—I think I put my hand on him. And he felt—" She shuddered. "He felt clammy. Real—real clammy. Like a—a wet rock, or something. So then I—I remember that I got real—real scared. Terrified. I—I suddenly felt like whoever killed him, they were still there, and they'd kill me. So then I—" She paused, blinking dull, unfocused eyes. Her voice had fallen to a low, dazed monotone. Reliving the experience, already narcotized by fatigue, she was slipping into mild shock.

"The next thing I knew," she said, "I—I was in his car. I mean, I was in it, and I didn't know how, or why, or what I was doing, really. I just knew that I—I had to get away from there before I got killed. So then, the next thing, I was already on the freeway, heading south. And Christ, I—"

"Why south? Why not north, or east?"

"Well, I guess I didn't want to—you know—go over any bridges, and pay toll, or anything."

"You didn't want to be seen, in other words."

"Yeah, I guesso. I mean, I just didn't know *what* I was doing. Not really. I didn't even really know I was on the freeway, for Christ's sake, until I was pulled over to the side of the road, and I was throwing up again. So then I—"

"Don't you remember taking King's keys and his wallet?" I interrupted sharply. "You *must* remember that. You remember everything else. You remember touching him the first time. Are you telling me that you remember touching him—how he felt—but you can't remember taking his keys?"

She doggedly, hopelessly shook her head. "I *don't,* though. I swear to Christ, I don't."

"Were you still drunk?"

"I—I guesso. I dunno."

I nodded as I looked her over, taking my time. Finally, pitching my voice to a casual note, I asked, "Are you wearing the same clothes you wore Tuesday night, Diane?"

She frowned at the question, dully perplexed. Then she stared

82

down at her wrinkled, grimy slacks. "Yeah. They're the same. Why?"

I glanced at Canelli. He was nodding solemnly.

"The reason I'm asking," I said, "is that if we can verify that you were wearing those clothes Tuesday night at The Shed, and if the lab can't find any evidence of blood, then it's possible that your only problem will be a rap for car theft."

"W—what'd you mean? What're you saying, anyhow?"

"I'm saying that your bedroom looked like a slaughterhouse, Diane. And if it's true that the murderer knifed Thomas King, then he—or she—got covered with blood. So if we test your clothes, we can—"

"But I didn't *kill* him. I already *told* you that. I already told you what happened. I—"

"No one voluntarily admits to murder, Diane. Not the murderer, anyhow." I pushed my chair back and nodded to Canelli, who stepped to the door and turned the lock.

"Inspector Canelli will process you. We'll take your clothes and test them. If you're lucky, you'll be out on bail tomorrow. For Grand Theft Auto."

She was still shaking her head as she stared at me with a kind of prim, wide-eyed outrage.

"By the way," I said, rising to my feet. "Are you sure that Jack Winship was at The Shed when you left?"

She nodded. "I'm sure. The bastard."

"Where could we find him?"

"Who? Jack?"

"Yes."

"I dunno. He—a lot of the time, whenever I had someone with me, he'd be around the neighborhood. Just hanging around, sleeping in his van."

"So you *did* expect someone, Tuesday night?"

"N—no. I *didn't*. I meant that—"

"You expected someone, Diane. You just said so."

"No," she moaned. "I didn't *mean* that. I just meant that we had a fight, Jack and me. So I didn't expect Jack at my place, that night. Usually, whenever we have a fight, it takes him a while to cool down. Me, too."

"Where do you think Winship went on Tuesday night, Diane? Let's assume that he didn't leave The Shed until after midnight. Where would he have gone?"

"Who knows? Christ, he could've gone anywhere. He's got that goddamn van. He could've gone anywhere. Anywhere but my place."

"All right." I signaled for Canelli to open the door. "I'll be talking to you later in the day, Diane."

"I'll bet you will." As she shuffled out, she threw me a last look of weary defiance.

Twelve

Friedman raised a broad, beefy hand. "It's on me. Want a doughnut, too?"

"No, thanks."

I carried both coffees to a table while Friedman carried his bearclaw. As he sat down opposite me, he said, "Do you realize that you're staring at my bearclaw?"

"That's because I disapprove."

"How about sugar?" He reached for the dispenser. "Do you disapprove of sugar?"

"That's right."

"Hmm." Freehand, he poured a thick crystalline sugar-stream into his coffee.

"They're discovering that sugar is linked to heart disease, you know."

"Hmm." He complacently stirred the coffee. Then: "You seem to have made out pretty well with Diane Farley."

"I think I got a straight story from her. It sounded straight, anyhow."

"The lab report will either kill her or cure her, assuming she wore those clothes the night of the murder."

"Right."

"Incidentally, the autopsy report is in on Thomas King. Did you see it?"

"No."

"There weren't any surprises, especially. The cause of death was three separate knife thrusts, two of which entered the heart. A good, clean job, in other words. The weapon was the switch-blade knife, no doubt about it. However—" He paused to bite into the butter-dripping bearclaw, then talked around the mouthful. "However, it turns out that there was a fractured vertebra at the base of the neck. According to the coroner, the victim could've been knocked out by the traditional round, blunt instrument before he was killed with the knife."

"If that's what really happened, then the actual killing—the knifing—could've been done execution-style."

"Right. Of course, that one little word—if—is responsible for sending lots of cops down lots of sour-smelling trails."

"What else did the coroner say?"

"He said that assuming the victim ate dinner between six and seven P.M., then he probably died between nine P.M. and midnight. Of course, that's approximate. Personally, in any case where the victim's been dead more than six hours, I just don't trust the time-of-death estimate. There's just too many variables. Even the body temperature, for God's sake, can be rigged."

"I wish we could find Jack Winship. I keep thinking that he could've driven to the apartment, killed King, and been gone by the time Diane Farley showed up."

Friedman frowned, then judiciously shook his head. "I don't buy it."

"Why not?"

"What's the motive? Jealousy?"

"Maybe."

"No way," he said.

"How can you say that? You haven't even laid eyes on Winship."

"Okay. I'll bet you a three-dollar lunch that it's not Winship. Want to bet?"

"No."

"See?" He finished the bearclaw, smacked his lips, and reached for his coffee.

"What I'd like to know," I said, "is who tipped us."

"Maybe it was Diane Farley. Did you ask her?"

"Not directly. But I know it wasn't her."

He shrugged, and for a moment we sat in silence while Friedman drank the last of his coffee.

"What're you going to do now?" he asked.

"I think I'll get Canelli, and go out and see Mrs. King."

"All right. Meanwhile, I'll see if I can't find Winship. If he's driving that van, he shouldn't be hard to find."

"Good idea."

"First, though, I think I'll have another bearclaw. Maybe you'd better leave, to spare yourself the spectacle."

"Maybe I should." I rose to my feet. "I'll be checking with you in an hour or so."

"Right. Good luck with the widow King."

Placing his misshapen hat on the sofa beside him, Canelli surveyed the living room with round, awed eyes. "This is some place," he stage-whispered. "I mean, this place could be on the cover of *House and Garden,* or somewhere."

Nodding agreement, I leaned toward him to say softly, "While I'm talking to Mrs. King, I want you to get the son—Bruce—and interrogate him. Find out what you can about how the father lived, and what kind of a home life they had."

"That kid looks like kind of a weirdo to me, Lieutenant. You know, real pale and jumpy, with those glittering eyes, and all. What if he starts to come unglued on me or something?"

"If he does, let it drop. We don't want to—"

Mrs. King was standing in the archway, facing us. Her simple black dress was expensively cut to accent a trim, taut, exciting body. She stood with chin raised, hands clasped tightly at her waist. Her dark eyes were shrewd and steady. Her brown hair was pulled back from a lean, uncompromising face. Markham had put her age at forty. It was a sensuous, sexually self-confident forty.

"I'm sorry to intrude, Mrs. King," I said, rising to my feet. "But there's certain information we've got to have if we're going to find your husband's murderer."

For a moment she didn't reply. Her eye didn't drop, her posture didn't shift. Then, speaking slowly and deliberately, she said, "There was another man here last night. Sergeant Markham. He was here for an hour, asking questions."

"I know that, Mrs. King. And I won't be that long, I promise you." As I said it, I stepped back, gesturing her to a chair. She hesitated a last long moment, then deliberately took another chair. As she settled herself, I asked permission for Canelli to interrogate Bruce. She made no objection.

I decided on a cryptic, businesslike approach. "Did your husband have any enemies, Mrs. King? Was there anyone who'd threatened him—anyone who bore him a grudge?"

Her eyes narrowed as she considered the question. She sat very erect, her back arched away from the chair. She didn't look at me as she shook her head in one short, decisive arc. "No one hated Tom. A lot of people didn't like him. But no one hated him."

"You're sure? Absolutely sure? We often find that someone will carry a grudge for years, especially if he's unbalanced." I paused, to let the point sink in. "Can you think of anyone in your husband's past who might have borne him a grudge?"

"No, I can't." It was a quick, cryptic retort—too quick to have allowed time for thought. Had she already searched her mind and her husband's past for clues? Or had she simply decided to be uncooperative?

Speaking slowly and deliberately, I said, "You're aware of the circumstances under which your husband was murdered, aren't you, Mrs. King?"

Looking straight ahead, she nodded. I saw her mouth tighten, her eyes harden. Beneath the pale, smooth flesh of her temple, a small muscle began to twitch.

"Were you aware that your husband had seen Miss Farley about once a week for a period of approximately six months?"

She turned her head to look at me directly. Deep in her eyes I saw a slowly kindling hostility. Her voice was brittle as she said, "Miss Farley is a model, Lieutenant. My husband was a film maker. Have you considered that?"

"Are you saying that you know of his—visits to Diane Farley?"

"No, I'm not saying that." Her voice was totally uninflected, as if she were reciting by rote. Her eyes revealed nothing.

"Are you aware that Miss Farley has been arrested on a morals charge, Mrs. King?"

Her lips curved in a wry smile. "Are you trying to shock me, Lieutenant? Because if you are, you aren't succeeding."

"You aren't shocked, then, at the possibility that your husband might've been having an affair with Diane Farley?"

Again she looked at me with her dark, intense eyes. The malevolence was plainer now—closer to the surface. But she still spoke with a slow, icy precision. "I had absolute confidence in my husband, Lieutenant. It's as simple as that. We both had separate careers. He spent a lot of time away from home. So do I. But we always trusted each other. That's the only way it could've worked. And it *did* work."

I allowed a moment of silence to pass before I said, "But now he's dead. Someone killed him. I want to find the murderer."

She didn't reply. But almost imperceptibly, her shoulders moved. She'd been about to shrug.

"I have to ask two more questions," I said in a brisker, more businesslike voice. "Then I'll let you go."

"All right."

"First, can you give me the approximate amounts of your husband's life insurance policies?"

"Yes. There was one policy for a hundred thousand dollars."

"Thanks." I rose to my feet, then waited for her to rise. As she did, I said casually, "The other question I have to ask, Mrs. King, is where you were on Tuesday evening. Were you home?"

Already turned toward the arch leading into the hallway, she stopped, then slowly pivoted to face me directly. "Are you asking me for an alibi, Lieutenant?" Her voice was dangerously low.

"Your husband was murdered in the apartment of a young woman who'd been arrested on a morals charge, Mrs. King. Until we know more about the whole matter, we have to assume that his presence at Diane Farley's apartment could've been a motive for an irate wife to commit murder. You say you trusted your husband, and I believe you. But I still have to ask these questions."

"My husband was murdered with a knife, Lieutenant. Are you telling me that I could have knifed my own husband? Struggled with him and knifed him?" She looked at me with silent contempt before saying, "You must be out of your mind."

I sighed. "Mrs. King, I've seen a two-hundred-pound man killed by a hundred-pound woman wielding an ashtray. Now, what I'm asking you is a completely routine question. I'm here to eliminate you as a suspect in your husband's death. And to do that, I've got to know where you were at the time of his death." I spread my hands. "It's simple logic."

She allowed a last moment of icy contempt to pass before she said, "I was delayed at the office until after eight."

"What company do you work for, Mrs. King?"

"Wetherby Associates. We import antiques. I'm the manager."

"I know the company. They're big. If you're their manager, then you must have a very good job."

She nodded. "I *do* have a good job."

"You said you spend a lot of time away from home."

"Yes. It's a wholesale business. I'm on the road about half the time."

"To get back to Tuesday, you probably got home, here, about eight thirty, assuming that you left Wetherby's at eight."

"Yes."

"Was your husband here when you arrived?"

"No. He called me about five, to say that he was working on a job and wouldn't be home until late."

"Did he say what the job was?"

"No, he didn't."

"Was your son here when you arrived home?"

"Yes."

"So the two of you—Bruce and you—were home all night."

"Yes. In fact, we were in bed before ten, asleep. We were both tired. We—"

From the hallway came the sharp sound of a ringing telephone. I heard footsteps hurrying from the back of the house. On the third ring, Bruce King answered the phone.

"It's for you, Mother. It's Uncle Harry. He wants to know about the funeral."

"Tell him it's tomorrow. It's— Wait. I'll talk to him." Moving with long, purposeful strides, she left the room. As she took the phone from the boy, I stepped into the hallway and beckoned Bruce King into the living room.

"Could I have a few words with you?" I asked softly.

He muttered diffident assent, then sat on the arm of a Victorian velvet sofa. He was a tall, loosely built boy with disheveled blond hair, a bad complexion and unsteady, unhappy eyes.

Speaking against the background of Mrs. King's terse, cryptic phone conversation, I said, "Is there anything you can tell me that might help us, Bruce? Anything at all?"

He first shrugged, then shook his head. It was a typically ambivalent teen-age mannerism, both pettishly annoyed and deeply aggrieved. "I already *talked* to the other one, you know. Inspector Canelli. I—I told him everything I could think of. *Everything*. I mean—" He paused, then said, "I mean, I thought it was a burglar, or something. At least—" His eyes slid toward the sound of his mother's voice. "At least, that's what *she* said."

He'd accented "she" with bitter derision. Was it merely a perverse adolescent's reaction to grief? Or was it something more?

I hesitated, then said, "You might not want to answer this, Bruce. And I couldn't blame you. But I've got to ask you anyway." I waited for his full attention. Then: "Would you say that your parents got along well? Or would you say that they fought more than most married couples?"

His pale, thin face suddenly convulsed. His voice was choked: "They were *past* fighting. They *tried* that. For years, they tried that. All during the time when I was little, that's all I can remember. I—I even used to have dreams about it. One dream, I used to have all the time. They'd be arguing—fighting, like they always did. And then their screams would turn into something solid, hanging in the air between them. They were like animal claws, those words, with blood dripping down. And then I'd see my parents. Both of them. And they—they'd both be all bloody. All torn up. Especially their faces. And—and—" Suddenly he gasped.

I got to my feet and turned to face him. From the hallway I could still hear Marjorie King's voice. "I'm sorry I had to ask," I said quietly. "But it's my job. Do you understand?"

Blindly, he nodded.

"I've just got one more question. It's about Tuesday night. I'd like to know what time you went to bed, Tuesday night."

Instead of replying, he only stared. His mouth worked impotently.

"What time, Bruce?" I asked quietly. "What time did you go to bed?"

"It—it was—was a little before ten. But—but—" He licked at his lips. "But why do you—" He couldn't finish it. He couldn't wrench his eyes from mine. His body had gone slack; his mouth hung slightly open. Sitting slumped on the arm of the velvet sofa, he was helpless.

I got slowly to my feet, reaching for my hat. "Thanks, Bruce," I said quietly. "That's all I need to know."

As I turned away, I heard him say, "Wh—what time was he—he killed?"

"We're not sure. Probably about ten thirty or eleven." I smiled at him, thanked him again, and left the room. I found Canelli in the dining room. He looked more than usually at odds with his surroundings, sitting lumpishly in a delicate Regency side chair. I motioned for him to remain seated, whispering that I was going to take a quick look through the large ground-floor flat. While I prowled, Canelli would keep the mother and son occupied.

Thirteen

"Where to, Lieutenant?" Canelli started the engine.

"Let's have a look at the victim's place of business." I glanced at my notebook. "It's 540 Bay Street. King Productions."

"Roger."

I checked in with Communications, got no messages, and advised them of our next stop. I flipped off the "transmit" switch and settled back in my seat. "What'd you get out of Bruce King?" I asked.

"Not much, really, Lieutenant. Except that he looks to me like one of those real screwed-up kids. I mean, I wouldn't be surprised if he was queer, you know? But, anyhow, he's sure uptight. I mean, he's *really* uptight."

I didn't comment, and we rode in silence for the next few blocks. I was thinking of Ann—and of her stricken face as she'd faced her husband the night before, receiving his curt instructions for the weekend. The boys were going skiing tomorrow, leaving at four P.M. A month ago, with a similar opportunity, we'd spent the weekend at Big Sur. We'd driven down the narrow seaside highway in the rain, leaving Friday night. We'd rented a small, shingled bungalow with a fieldstone fireplace and a four-poster bed. We'd gone shopping before we'd left San Francisco, buying four huge sacks of steaks and fruit, bacon and eggs, French bread and wine. We'd . . .

". . . you find out from Mrs. King?" Canelli was asking. "Anything new?"

"I don't know," I answered. "I can't figure her out."

"She sure don't look much like a grief-stricken widow."

"I don't think she *is* very grief-stricken."

"What were you looking for when you went over the flat just before we left?"

"I was trying to get an idea of the layout. She said that both she and Bruce were in bed by ten o'clock, Tuesday. Asleep, supposedly."

"Hey," he said slowly. "Hey, she could have sneaked out. Is that what you're thinking, Lieutenant?"

"I'm thinking that either one of them could have sneaked out."

He whistled. "You mean the kid? Bruce? You mean he could've done it?"

"Mrs. King says that she couldn't have stabbed her husband. Physically, she claims, she couldn't've done it. And she's probably right. It's a messy job, stabbing someone. Women usually don't use knives. Not unless they're in a frenzy, and then they hack—and they keep hacking. But a teen-age boy, a little off his rocker, might've done it. He'd have had the strength. And, assuming that he was infuriated by his father's affair with Diane Farley, he'd have had the motive."

"What about that blow to the neck, though? King could've been already knocked out when he was stabbed. That'd make the whole deal a lot neater. I mean, the stabbing wouldn't've been so tough, then, for a woman to do."

"Yes," I answered thoughtfully, "you're right, Canelli. That would've made it a lot neater." I pointed to the next intersection. "Turn there. We'll hit Bay Street just right."

"Oh. Yeah." He wrenched the cruiser into an abrupt turn. "Say, what about Diane Farley, Lieutenant? What's with her, anyhow?"

"When The Shed opens this evening, we'll see whether we can verify what clothes she was wearing Tuesday night. If she was wearing the same clothing she's got on now, and if the lab doesn't find any traces of blood, then I'm inclined to believe her story. She got home, found the body, panicked, and started running."

Canelli doubtfully shook his head. "I don't know, Lieutenant. I mean, San Diego's a long way to run."

"Yes, but she was driving north when she was picked up. And don't forget, she'd been drinking. She was scared, too—afraid she might be murdered. Also, she's been arrested once. I've noticed that a certain type of person, if they've fallen once, they seem to become irrational at the idea of any contact with the police. That could've been her problem, complicated by alcohol. It's crazy. But it happens."

"Well, maybe." Plainly, he wasn't convinced. But, with transparent diplomacy, he decided to change the subject. "What about Jack Winship? What's with him?"

"That's exactly what I'm wondering. Which is another reason for checking out The Shed. I want to know when Jack Winship left, and where he went." I pointed ahead. "Park there, by the hydrant. 540 Bay is just around the corner."

"Oh. Right."

King Productions was a large storefront building tastefully converted into better-paying commercial property. An overweight brunette presided over a small reception room dominated by huge photo murals of San Francisco. When I showed her the shield, the brunette immediately heaved a deep, theatrical sigh. Her chin began to quiver—experimentally, I thought.

"I guess you want to see Mr. Mallory," she said heavily. "He's the manager. I mean, I guess he's in charge, now that poor Mr. King is—is—" She gulped, and began blinking tears into her eyes.

"Fine. I'll talk to Mr. Mallory."

She spoke briefly into the phone, then pointed to a door. "You go right through there, Lieutenant." She paused, still blinking. "I think it's awful," she offered. "About Mr. King, I mean. Just simply awful."

I looked at her speculatively, then gestured to Canelli. If she was anxious to talk, Canelli could listen.

Mallory's office looked as if it was part of a set, hastily partitioned off from the bustle of a sound stage. Mallory was waiting for me, leaning gracefully in the open doorway. He was a slim, elegant man of about thirty-five. He was modishly dressed in flared slacks, a paisley-printed sports shirt and expensive Wellington boots—the same style boots that Thomas King had worn Tuesday night. I watched Mallory fussily clear off the office's single straight-backed visitor's chair.

"I'm sorry," he said testily. "All this—this commotion. This *confusion*. I can't *think*, much less get anything accomplished. It's just—just—" Fluttering a hand, he let the thought go unfinished as he slumped down behind a piled-high desk. He pushed his pink-tinted aviator's glasses up on his nose, and ran long, graceful fingers through reddish, ringleted hair. "Did you know that someone else was here, not more than two hours ago?" He frowned. "Markham. Sergeant Markham."

I smiled at him. "Unfortunately, Mr. Mallory, police work is ninety percent repetition. We go back over the same ground, time after time. Eventually we get lucky."

The last phrase startled him. He glanced at me, then looked quickly away, momentarily disconcerted. "Good," he murmured, quickly recovering. Then: "Does that mean you—you've discovered who killed him?" As he asked the question, he couldn't quite meet my eyes.

"We're still checking." I allowed a moment of silence to pass. Then: "Is there any way you can help me, Mr. Mallory?"

"Me?" At first he smiled. Then, fleetingly, he frowned, elaborately puzzled—playacting, perhaps. "Me? How can I help?"

"Very simple. Just tell me about Thomas King. How was he to work for? What kind of a film maker was he? Did he pay his bills? Did he keep his word? How were his morals? How was his bank account?" I spread my hands invitingly. "Everything and anything. It might not seem important to you. But it's possible that we can combine it with something else."

As he'd listened, his eyes first went blank, then refocused on me with dawning recognition. "You were on TV last night, weren't you? I *thought* I recognized you."

"That's right, Mr. Mallory." Deliberately, I said nothing more. He glanced at me with transparent speculation, then cleared his throat, at the same time frowning—ostentatiously puzzled. "Yes. Well—" Again he cleared his throat. "Well, it's, ah, difficult for me to know exactly how much to say. I mean—" He pushed up the glasses and again caressed the elaborately arranged hair. "I mean, I know there's such a thing as defamation of character. And I wouldn't want to—"

"Not when you're talking to a police officer, Mr. Mallory. In fact, it works in reverse. We want to hear everything. The works. If you hold back information, you're actually committing a crime."

"Yes. Certainly. I'm aware of that, naturally. However, I'm sure you want facts. As opposed to opinions, I mean—unsubstantiated hearsay. You don't want that, do you?" His sidelong glance was almost coy.

"If you identify it as opinion, Mr. Mallory, there's no problem. And there's never any possibility of libel when you're talking with an officer. There's no problem about anonymity either. I'm sure you understand that. We protect our sources. That's our first rule."

"Yes. Well, of course I see the movies and everything. But that's not always quite the same thing as—" He broke off, frowning down at the desk. Then: "What if there's a trial, though? Would I have to testify?"

"That's up to the D.A. However, the D.A. takes our recommendations. Naturally, we work together."

"Yes. Naturally. I mean, I'm sure you do. Still—" He doubtfully shook his head.

I decided to edge my voice with the chill of authority. "Why don't you just start talking, Mallory? Let's see what kind of information—or opinions—you've got, before we start worrying about what you're going to say on the witness stand. That's a long, long way in the future, believe me."

"Yes. Well, of course, I can see *that*. And of course I want to do my duty." He coughed delicately, at the same time covertly measuring me with another coy look. "Yes," he repeated, nodding. As he nodded, the glasses slipped down on his nose. "You're right. No doubt about it. None at all." He pushed at the glasses with a languid forefinger.

"So just start talking," I said shortly. "The sooner we start, the sooner we can finish, and you can get back to work."

The remark sent his soft brown eyes to the cluttered desk. His mouth pursed into a fretful pout as he murmured something about the rigors of paperwork. Finally, with a last limp gesture of resignation, he began talking. "You asked me how Mr. King was to work for," he said. "Well"—he sighed deeply, shaking his head with bogus reluctance—"well, to be completely candid, Lieutenant, he was awful—*simply* awful. I mean, in the first place, I don't think he could make a one-minute TV spot if his *life* depended on it. He could get the business, all right. I'll say *that* for him. He was a salesman. He could sell anything, no doubt about it. But technically, he was impossible. *Simply* impossible. I mean, he used to come up with these *utterly* outlandish ideas that he'd already sold to his client. And then he'd tell me to execute them. Just like *that*." He snapped his fingers. "It was ludicrous. *Simply* ludicrous."

"How long have you worked for him, Mr. Mallory?"

"Nine years. Nine long, hard years. Before I came here, I was with Disney. And why I left, I'll never know."

"Was Mr. King successful in business, would you say?"

"You mean monetarily successful? Is that what you mean?"

"Yes, that's what I mean."

"Well, then, the answer is yes. He made lots of money. However, he made it at the expense of others."

"You, for instance."

"Yes," he answered, aggrieved. "Since you said it, I won't deny it. *Yes*." The brown eyes were harder now. The rosebud mouth was malicious. "I won't deny it," he repeated. "He fed me on promises. And I fell for them. *All* of them. Time after time. Year after year. First I was going to have a piece of the business. Then I was going to be manager. Finally I was going to be a partner."

"But you *are* the manager. And he relied on your talent. You said so yourself."

As he smothered an obscenity, he jerked his hand up from the desk to circle the four walls. "Look at this—this *hovel*," he hissed. "*Look* at it. Have you seen *his* office?"

"No."

"Well—" He flounced back hard in his chair. "Well, if you had, you'd know what I'm *talking* about."

I tried to register a sympathetic interest, shaking my head sadly. Then I said, "As far as you know, then, Mr. King's affairs were in order. He apparently made plenty of money, and he wasn't in trouble financially."

"Oh, he was in good *financial* shape, all right. I won't take *that* away from him. He was shrewd." Mallory nodded decisively. "He was one hell of a shrewd operator. No question."

"And he wasn't being pressed by creditors that you know of."

"No. Never. As I say, he had his faults. *Plenty* of them. But bad money management wasn't one of them. At least not in business. What he did with his personal finances, of course, I don't know."

"Do you know Diane Farley, Mr. Mallory?"

"Diane who?"

"Farley. Diane Farley. It was in her apartment that Mr. King was murdered."

The eyes were suddenly avid. "He was murdered in a girl's apartment?"

"Didn't Sergeant Markham tell you?"

"No"—he blinked—"no, he didn't."

"Miss Farley is a model. That's why I thought you might know her."

He frowned. "What kind of a model?"

"I'm not sure," I lied. "Fashion, I think."

"Well, I don't know her. But I can tell you that King saw lots of girls. All kinds of girls. At all hours of the day—and night."

I flattened my voice, saying matter-of-factly, "He played around. Is that what you mean?"

His smile was sly. "Under oath, I might deny it, Lieutenant. But, yes, that's what I'm saying. King was constantly trailing off after women. Or, more accurately, girls. He was forty-three, you know, and he couldn't keep his eyes off girls, much less his hands. Mostly young girls, and the more—curves, the better." Involuntarily, his voice revealed a scornful distaste for women and their curves.

"So it wouldn't surprise you to learn that Thomas King slept with Diane Farley once a week."

He snorted. "It would surprise me if he *hadn't*. Not with Diane Farley, especially. I didn't even know her, as I said. But he could've slept with anyone—and everyone."

"What about his wife? Mrs. King. Do you know her?"

"Well, naturally I know her." The contempt was back in his voice—and in his eyes.

"Did you know anything about their life—their private life?"

"I know that she played around as much as he did," he said promptly. "They were meant for each other. Two of a kind."

"You're *sure* that she played around?"

"Well, of course"—he bridled—"I don't know whether she actually *slept* with other men. I mean, there's no way I could *know* that, not for sure. But I've seen her with other men. According to the stories, she played some pretty strange games. She looks very proper, you know—very straight. But those are the ones, you know, who can really fool you. Just last month, for instance, I saw her having drinks with a man who *couldn't* have been more than twenty-five. Maybe he was twenty, for all I know. Not only that, but he was really far-out—really bizarre. Appearance-wise, any-how. Naturally, I didn't talk to them."

"Do you know this man's name, Mr. Mallory?"

"No."

"Do you remember the bar?"

"Yes. It was the Pelican, on Clement Street."

"Did you ever see her with anyone—a man—that you could identify?"

"Well, no. Not really. Not by name, anyhow."

I nodded, thought about it, and then decided to ask, "What about Tuesday, Mr. Mallory? Was there any change in Thomas King's normal schedule on Tuesday?"

He thoughtfully touched the tip of a small pink tongue to his upper lip, then shook his head. "Nothing," he answered. "He came in about nine thirty in the morning, shuffled a few papers and made a few phone calls. Then he went out to see a client. That was about ten, I suppose. He came back about three, I guess it was. And he left about five. It was his typical working day," Mallory said contemptuously.

"He didn't come back to the office that evening?"

"No."

"Would you have known it, if he'd come back?"

"Probably. For one thing, I was here myself until almost eight. I was working on a presentation that he needed by yesterday. Wednesday. That's the way it went, you see. That's what I'm *telling* you: He went home at five. I stayed till eight. It's typical. *Utterly* typical."

"What did you do after you left here Tuesday evening, Mr. Mallory?"

"I had something to eat, and a couple of drinks. Then I went home." He hesitated, then said, "Is that what you're asking? Are you—" He licked at his cupid's lips, suddenly frowning. "Are you asking me what I was doing Tuesday night?"

I held his eye as I slowly, silently nodded. Immediately, his acid-tongued arrogance began to fail him. "Well—" He defensively spread his hands. "I just—as I said—I just had an omelette, actually, and a split of wine. And then I—I went home. I got home about eleven. Or may—maybe a little before. I—I'm not sure. I mean, I—" As he broke off, he turned both palms upward, then dropped his hands to the desk top.

"Do you live alone, Mr. Mallory?"

"Well"—he coughed—"well, no. I mean, I have a roommate. But Tuesday he was out of town. So I can't—"

His telephone rang. With obvious relief, he answered. Then, surprised, he handed the phone to me.

"It's Pete, Frank," Friedman said. "Can you talk?"

"More or less."

"Well, I wanted to tell you about a couple of things."

"Yes." I took out my notebook.

"First, they've located Winship's van. The call just came in. Just this minute. It's down in Pacifica. It's parked right near the beach—right off Route One."

"Empty?"

"It's empty, all right. It's parked in among some scrub trees, apparently. However, the door was found open, as if someone had left in a hurry. Also, there's some blood on the ground. So the tension builds, as they say."

"I'll go down for a look."

"Yeah. Fine. However, hurry back. Because I've just heard from Sacramento on those fingerprints on the murder weapon. And guess what?"

"What?"

"They belong to Arnold Clark." He paused, then asked, "Are you acquainted with Arnold Clark?"

"No."

"I guess he took his best shots before you joined the team. Anyhow, I can tell you that we may have our work cut out for us."

"Listen," I said, glancing at Mallory. "I can't—"

"Okay. Sorry. Why don't you run down to Pacifica for a quick look at the van, and then get back here to the Hall as soon as you can? I'll get Markham down here, too. Just take a quick look at the terrain, and try to make it here in, say, an hour. Okay?"

"Yes. Fine. Will you dispatch the technicians?"

"There, we got a break—money-wise, anyhow. The van was found just over the county line. So San Mateo's going to supply the crews."

"All right. I'll try to see you in an hour."

Fourteen

Canelli pulled in behind a San Mateo County Sheriff's car. I cleared our own car with San Francisco Communications, and we stepped out onto a narrow dirt road. No more than two tire ruts, the road led into a seaside grove of twisted, wind-stunted juniper. I could understand why it had taken twenty-four hours to locate Winship's van. The area where we now stood was bleak and deserted, an underbrush-tangled slope dropping steeply down to the rocky shoreline, far below. Only during the warmest months of the year would hikers venture into this rough terrain. At the thought, I turned up my collar against the raw winter's wind.

A deputy sheriff checked our credentials, then led us to the van. It tallied perfectly with Judy Blake's description: color, body condition, rust spots and the unmistakable smokestack, cocked at a crazy angle. I wondered whether it had purposely been bent into that Toonerville shape.

The van's interior was dirty and cluttered. A tattered sleeping bag was spread out on a plywood panel that had been covered with a foam-rubber pad, badly stained. A cardboard box of canned food lay on the floor beside another box filled with tools, cans of oil and miscellaneous Volkswagen parts. The car's upholstery was worn and ripped. The odometer registered 4,000 miles, translating to 104,000.

105

Querying the deputy, I learned that the van had been found less than two hours ago. It had only been in the past hour, when the blood was found, that San Mateo had organized a search for Winship. At about that time, someone had remembered our A.P.B., and advised San Francisco Communications. The technical crews hadn't arrived, but the deputy assured me they were on their way.

"How many men have you got in the area?" I asked the deputy.

"Searching for the driver, you mean?"

I nodded.

"Well, I'd say about—" He calculated, frowning heavily. "I'd say about eight. Maybe nine. I mean, our department don't exactly have unlimited resources, you know, Lieutenant. I mean, we've got to—"

"Can you show me where the blood was found? I'm in kind of a hurry."

"Oh. Right. Sure thing. It's right here, Lieutenant. Right over here." He pointed down the narrow road.

I told Canelli to stay with our radio and followed the squat, bandy-legged deputy down the sharp slope of the road. About twenty-five feet from the car, we came to a break in the thick-growing scrub. A precarious footpath led down to the rocky beach, a hundred feet below. The deputy took the path, needlessly warning me to watch my footing. At the first bend, he stooped and pointed out an unmistakable smear of blood on a cluster of ice plant.

"So far," he said, "that's all we've found. But like I say, it's only been an hour since—"

Holstered at his belt, his walkie-talkie beeped.

"Blakely," he barked officiously. "Come in."

"We found him," a metallic voice said. "Or, anyhow, we found somebody. Dead."

"Where?"

"Just go down the path. We can see you, from where we are. He's down in the rocks, here, about fifty feet up from the surf. Just keep a-coming, and we'll tell you where to turn."

Blakely shot me a self-satisfied look, then turned and led the way down.

Again, Judy Blake's description had been accurate. Winship looked as she'd described him: greasy-haired, pimply-faced, dressed in tatters. Tumbled among a pile of black, lichen-crusted boulders, he lay with his arms and legs spread wide, his broken torso wedged tightly between two boulders. His mouth was open wide, as if he were screaming for help. All of his front teeth were broken; one lens of his glasses was shatter-starred. He wore a dirty yellow sweat shirt stained by two saucer-size patches of dried blood. Centered in each stain was a bullet hole.

Looking up toward the path, I could plainly see broken branches that marked his fall. He must have fled down the road to the footpath, where he'd been shot. The impact of the bullets could easily have pitched him crashing down the slope.

I turned toward the bandy-legged deputy. He was staring down at the body. His normally ruddy face was greenish now.

"Is your name Blakely?"

"Y—yessir."

"Are you in command here?"

"Well, I—" He swallowed. With some effort, he wrenched his gaze away from the body. "I—I guesso," he said finally. Then, blinking, he nodded. "Yeah, I'm in charge."

"Are you sure your lab crew is on the way?"

He blinked again, focusing his eyes vaguely. "Yeah. Sure. Th—they were going to fingerprint the van. You know—to find out who stole it."

"All right. Good. Now, in addition, you'll need the coroner. And you'd better organize an inch-by-inch search of the area around the van and down the road to the footpath where we saw the blood. The assailant may have used an automatic weapon, and the shell casing might be in the underbrush. Also, you'll want to keep everyone off the road and the path until the area's been photographed. *Completely* photographed. That's vital. And, of course, you'll want to photograph him." I pointed to the corpse.

"Oh. Yeah. Of course."

I looked closely at the deputy. As he stood irresolutely staring down at the victim, Blakely was again turning pale. He was swallowing rapidly; his brows were gathering in a perplexed frown. I touched his shoulder. Slowly, he turned to face me. His eyes were dull. His mouth hung slightly open.

Lowering my voice and stepping very close, I pointed up the slope. "Get up to your car," I ordered, "and put in a call for your superior officer. Tell him to come to your assistance. Immediately. Tell him that it's my request. I've got to get back to the city, fast, but I'm going to leave Inspector Canelli with you. Until your superior arrives, I want you to do exactly as Canelli says. He's an experienced homicide officer, and he'll take full responsibility." I paused. Then, speaking very softly and very distinctly, I said, "You'd better not screw up any evidence here, Blakely. Because if you do, it's your ass. Do you understand?"

As I spoke, I watched him closely. When I saw his eyes clearing with the first spark of anger, I repeated the threat, then turned abruptly away and began climbing the rocky hillside.

Fifteen

"Here." Friedman sailed a B.C.I.D. report across his desk. "For openers, read that. Then you can tell me about your adventures in Pacifica."

The report was headed "Fingerprint Classification, Knife (switchblade type), Homicide (King, Thomas A.)." Sacramento had tentatively identified the two "80 percent prints" as belonging to Arnold Clark, a convicted felon. After the usual disclaimer that the prints could be used only for guidance, not in evidence, the report described Clark as thirty-six years old, black, with one conviction for aggravated assault and another for rape. He'd been in San Quentin for nine of the past ten years, and on parole for nine months. During those months, he'd been clean. Clark's present address was given as 549 Hayes Street, San Francisco.

As I passed the report to Markham, I said to Friedman, "Clark could be the black man leaving the scene of the crime."

"Could be," Friedman agreed blandly. Then: "You said you weren't acquainted with Arnold Clark."

"No." I pointed to the report. "He went to 'Q' about the time I started working here."

"That's right. I keep forgetting that you were playing football while most of us were earning an honest living. Well—" He waved his cigar ash vaguely toward an overflowing ashtray, missing the tray by six inches. "Well, the plain fact is that Arnold Clark is a king-size pain in the ass. A hundred more like him, and we'd be hit with mass resignations. Believe it."

Irritated at Friedman's theatrics—and at the nagging realization that I should recognize Clark's name—I curtly pointed out that as a parolee, Clark was clean.

"I didn't say he's stupid," Friedman countered. "I said he's a pain the ass. He's been lying low for nine months, that's all. But he hasn't been clean, you can bet on that. He's found a foolproof hustle. Clark and I have been doing business together for a long, long time—beginning when he was a nasty-acting teen-ager and I was a scared-ass patrolman, stuck down in the Fillmore. And I remember that Clark was always smart. He always had flair. If his peer group was clouting Ford and Chevy hubcaps, Clark would specialize in Cads. By the time I made inspector, Clark was an operator. Whatever he got into, he always made sure he got his right off the top. And in the meantime, he also developed a considerable talent for making it with white girls, since he's also very good-looking, in addition to being very smart and very tough. So naturally Clark was right on top of the 'Black is Beautiful' thing, just like he was on top of everything else, including black militancy. He got onto the radical chic skam, and made a good thing of it—as always. The only catch is that the real black militants—the Panthers, for instance—they won't have a thing to do with Clark and Company. To them, Clark is just a smart, opportunistic thug who has sense enough to wear tight pants."

"He can't be too smart. He fell twice."

"He was probably framed on that rape charge," Friedman said airily. "You know how it is. Pretty soon guys like Clark become a departmental embarrassment. Also, the judge gets tired of seeing them around, cluttering up his calendar. So we frame them, and the judge puts them away, and the indeterminate-sentence racket takes care of the rest. It's not justice, of course. But it's—"

"Look at this, Lieutenant." Markham had been reading through Clark's bulging jacket. Now Markham leaned avidly forward, turning a recent interrogation report for Friedman to see. "Read that." It was as much an order as a suggestion. Reluctantly, I realized that Markham had found something important. While Friedman was expostulating, Markham had been digging.

Grimacing, Friedman reached for his reading glasses. He cheerfully admitted to the vice of obesity, but not to middle-aging farsightedness.

Friedman read the report, whistled and passed the folder across to me.

Five months ago, I read, Clark had been picked up for questioning in a combined Vice and Narco raid. Clark had been charged with being in a place where drugs were used and where a lewd show was in progress. But the charges had been subsequently dropped. The location had been Emile Zeda's self-styled Satanic Temple. Clark's companion, according to the report, had been Marjorie King.

"Now there," Friedman said thoughtfully, "is a parley that boggles the mind. Mrs. Thomas King, wife of a philandering film maker. Arnold Clark, one of San Francisco's foremost hoods. And Emile Zeda, who gets rich titillating his faithful flock of Satan worshipers with the joys of pot-smoking and sex." As he pocketed his reading glasses, he dolefully shook his head. "Jesus, here we've been politely interrogating Mrs. King, the bereaved widow, and it turns out that we've already got a *file* on her, for God's sake. If the captain ever hears about this one . . ." He let it go unfinished.

"We may or may *not* have a file on her," I corrected. "As I remember that bust, there were a couple of society figures involved. The whole thing died pretty quick. Which is probably the reason that Clark's parole wasn't revoked."

Friedman picked up the phone, got Records, and asked for anything we had on Marjorie King. Then, settling back in his oversize swivel chair, his composure recovered, he grunted, "Which way do you bet, Frank? Is there a file on Marjorie King, or isn't there? Will virtue triumph, or corruptness? Personally"—he squinted up at the ceiling—"personally, I'll bet on virtue. With suitable odds, of course."

Ignoring his banter, I said thoughtfully, "Charles Mallory said that Marjorie King had some pretty bizarre playmates. But I figured he was just gossiping."

Markham snorted. "Charles Mallory plays some pretty funny games himself. In fact, the Vice Squad might have a file on *him*, too."

Friedman whistled again. "My God, I thought we had a white-collar homicide here. But it turns out that we're dealing with a bunch of crooks and thugs. What'd Mallory fall for?"

"He was picked up in a sweep of a gay bar," Markham said. "But he wasn't held. He was just driven around the block. That's why I'm not sure whether the Vice Squad has a file on him or not."

"How'd you hear about it, then?" I asked.

"I got it from the receptionist at King Productions." Markham permitted himself a thin, humorless smile. "That's a real wild place. Everyone hates everyone else. Miss Phillips, the receptionist, hates Mallory. And Mallory hates—hated—King."

"Who'd King hate?" Friedman asked.

Markham shrugged. "No one, as far as I could find out. Mallory thought that King was screwing him blind. But it turns out that, in his will, King left half the business to his wife, and half to Mallory."

"Are you sure of that?" I asked.

Markham's sidelong glance was patronizing. "I've got a Xerox copy of the will in my desk drawer. The court order came through about eleven this morning, authorizing us to open his safe-deposit box."

"Did Mallory know about that will?" Friedman asked.

I shook my head, but Markham nodded. "According to Miss Phillips, he did know about it."

I realized that I'd been outmaneuvered. Like a fool, I hadn't taken advantage of the fifteen minutes' ride down to Pacifica to quiz Canelli about his conversation with the receptionist. I'd assumed that it had been a fruitless interrogation. So, relaxing, Canelli and I had talked about football. We'd . . .

A single knock sounded, and Friedman's door opened. A rookie patrolman entered, placed a folder on Friedman's desk, smiled uncertainly and withdrew.

Friedman glanced at the single sheet of paper fixed to the jacket's manila folder. "By God, she *was* picked up, all right. Friday, October fourth." He flipped to a second sheet, doubtless a photocopy of the general complaint. "There were eighteen of Zeda's ever-loving Satan worshipers picked up, plus Zeda himself, plus two so-called altar assistants, plus the nudie stretched out on the altar, so called." He turned back to the first sheet. "Mrs. King wasn't held. Clark was the only one held. Which is what comes of being an ex-con. However, since the drug charge was apparently dropped, Clark's parole wasn't revoked."

"How about Zeda and company?" I asked. "Were they charged?"

Friedman smiled gently. "Unless I'm mistaken, the D.A. declined to prosecute on the very sensible grounds that the taxpayers weren't paying him to do public relations work for Emile Zeda. In fact, unless I'm again very much mistaken, Zeda's only beef was with the ASPCA."

"The ASPCA?"

"Right. Don't you remember that flap about Zeda's real live panther? He kept it tranquilized, and used it as a prop for his performances."

Markham balefully shook his head. "It really burns me, how shysters like Zeda can operate. He's nothing but a goddamn con man."

"He can operate simply because his customers want to be taken," Friedman replied. "And what's more, they can *afford* to be taken. So where's the harm?"

I placed Arnold Clark's jacket on top of Marjorie King's. "We're wasting time," I said shortly. "We've got Clark's prints on the murder weapon, for God's sake. What're we doing sitting here?"

"A good point," Friedman observed. "However, when you roust Arnold Clark, you'll discover that life is a lot more comfortable sitting around here and gossiping about Emile Zeda." He lit a cigar, taking his time. "Also," he continued, "you haven't told me about Winship."

"He's dead." I rose to my feet. "Shot. That's about all I can tell you. I had to leave Canelli down at Pacifica, because no one from San Mateo seemed to know what the hell they were doing. I don't think the officer in charge had ever seen a homicide victim before."

"Well, well, good for Canelli. This will probably be the making of him." Friedman drew deeply on the cigar, getting it satisfactorily lit. Then: "I'd offer my assistance rousting Clark," he said equably, "but I expect I'd better wait for Canelli's report, assuming he remembers to *make* a report. Besides, I've got a line on the bartender at The Shed. And I suppose, since Winship's dead, that we'd better find out exactly what he was doing Tuesday night."

"I suppose so." I gestured Markham toward the door.

Sixteen

"What the hell's keeping Culligan?" Markham said irritably. "It's been almost five minutes."

Not replying, I checked the walkie-talkie, lying on the seat between us. Had I mistakenly assigned Culligan to one channel, then turned to another? Had I . . .

"Lieutenant Hastings?" It was Culligan's voice.

I picked up the radio. "Yes. Are you and Sigler in position?"

"Roger," Culligan answered laconically.

"Can you see anything inside Arnold Clark's apartment?"

"No, sir. The kitchen's the only window we can see."

"Are you being observed?"

"We sure are. We've got no place to hide back here. We're just standing in the goddamn courtyard. One kid's already tried to drop some garbage on us."

I smiled. "Well, hang in there, Culligan. Sergeant Markham and I are going right up. Keep your eyes open."

"Yessir."

I handed the walkie-talkie to Markham, and we got out of the cruiser on opposite sides. We'd parked across the street from Clark's apartment building. As we stood on the curb, waiting for traffic to clear, I looked up and down the sidewalk. Already, I knew, our presence on the street had been discovered. Certain figures had slipped from sight, as quickly and naturally as small animals disappear into the underbrush at the first approach of a predator. Other figures were surreptitiously standing so as to keep us constantly in view. This was the ghetto: refuse-choked, despair-dogged, deadly dangerous. In these hostile streets a cop could suddenly die.

Walking side by side, we crossed to the far side of the street. I moved with slow, measured deliberation. At that moment, in that place, I was The Man. My power was immense. A touch of a walkie-talkie button, and a dozen armed men would arrive.

Yet a single bullet, fired from any doorway, could cancel that power.

As we walked, we constantly shifted our eyes, searching for the first flicker of alien movement. Our mannerisms were studied, seemingly remote. Predators must move according to fixed, time-less conventions, displaying neither haste nor fear. Momentarily my eye caught Markham's. Riding in the car with him—talking with him in the office—I disliked Markham. He disliked me. But now I must depend upon him—and I did. He could save my life—and would.

Our destination was a large frame apartment building. Originally built in the early 1900's for the carriage trade, the building was now in the final stages of decay. The cracked marble walls of the foyer were glazed with a thick patina of accumulated grime. There were twelve mailboxes, all of them with broken locks. On Hayes Street, most mail was never received.

We'd already determined that Clark's apartment was number six, second floor, rear.

"Let's go," I said.

Nodding, Markham began climbing the stairs. At the first land-ing, he unbuttoned his coat and loosened his revolver in its spring holster. It was Markham's responsibility to search for danger ahead. Following him, I would keep watch behind.

Surprisingly, the second-floor hallway had been newly carpeted in a cheap, garish red nylon. The walls were freshly painted. By ghetto standards, despite the building's decayed exterior, this was luxury. Only the downstairs foyer had been abandoned to the hoodlums and the hustlers. Yet the tenement odors remained: stale cooking, urine and an indelible mustiness. And already the new carpeting was burned and ripped, the fresh paint defaced by abuse and graffiti.

The door of apartment six was alone at the rear of the hallway. Clark's apartment, then, was probably larger than the others.

The knob was on the door's left side. As the ranking officer, it was my responsibility to actually open the door. Therefore, Markham stepped to the right, with his hand on his gun. He stood clear of the door.

I pushed the bell button, then stepped to the left. The butt of my revolver was reassuring in my hand.

Footsteps were approaching—light, cautious footsteps.

"Who is it?" The voice was low and husky. He was standing close behind the door, speaking softly.

"Arnold Clark?"

"That's right."

"Police. Open it up."

"You got a warrant?"

"You're a parolee, Clark. We don't need a warrant."

"You don't have a warrant, I don't open up."

Behind me, down the hallway, I could hear a door opening—then another. Markham was turning, to cover us.

"If you don't open that door, Clark, you're refusing to obey the lawful command of a police officer. That's a violation of your parole."

"So break it in, pig."

"No, we won't break it in. But if we have to get a warrant, it's your ass. You'll go back to 'Q.' Automatically. Now, I've told you what I'm going to do. You've got ten seconds to decide. You can stay on the street, or you can go back inside—just for what you decide to do in the next ten seconds. Your choice."

"What'd you want to talk about?"

"I'm starting to count."

Five seconds later, the lock clicked and the door opened.

"Well?" He wore only white undershorts and a barbarian's necklace: mismatched beads and curved animal teeth, all strung on a leather thong. He stood with legs spread wide, fists clenched on his hips. He was magnificently muscled, with thick arms, heavy shoulders and a hard, flat stomach. He wore a close-cropped beard, streaked with gray. His smooth-shaven skull glistened in the dim light of the hallway. A slim golden earring pierced the lobe of his left ear.

"Inside, Clark." I'd given up my grip on the gun butt. I stood with my arms loose at my sides, ready. I watched him smile, saw him step back a single slow, insolent pace.

"We can talk here, man. We're inside. That's what you wanted."

"I don't stand in hallways, Clark. Besides"—I looked him up and down—"besides, there's a draft."

"Yeah. Well, a draft is all right with me, if it's all right with you. And anyhow"—he moved his head back down the hallway—"anyhow, I've got a little—company."

"A woman?"

He slowly nodded, covertly watching me. Illicit sexual relations constituted parole violation.

"Inside, Clark."

He raised his stevedore's shoulders, sighed, shook his head and finally turned, giving way. Behind me, Markham closed the door and locked it. As I followed Clark down the hallway, I heard Markham on the walkie-talkie. Culligan and Sigler would return to their car, where they'd watch the front entrance.

Quickly surveying Clark's living room, I decided that he must have spent thousands on the furnishings. The outsize couch was covered with zebra skins, the walls were hung with African trophies: shields, spears, tribal masks. In contrast, some of the furniture was modern: burnished chrome, combined with oil-rubbed hardwoods. Elaborate hi-fi components were fitted into an intricately carved Mexican chest.

Long Way Down

Clark moved to a black leather safari chair and seated himself with deliberate, graceful insolence. I watched the play of his muscles. It would take four good men to subdue Clark.

The apartment was spacious: a living room, a kitchen and two bedrooms. The rooms were large, in good repair, newly painted. Behind a decaying ghetto façade, Clark was living in style.

Leaving Markham with his eye on Clark, I checked the kitchen, the bath and the front bedroom. All of them were in fair order, all of them furnished with a flamboyant, far-out flair. In the back bedroom, tangled in the blankets of a king-sized bed, I found a blonde. She looked to be in her early twenties, and she lay with the bedclothing drawn up tightly beneath her chin. She was very pale. She looked at me with huge, frightened eyes.

"Do you have any clothes on?" I asked.

She mutely shook her head.

"Well, put something on—anything. Then come into the living room."

"B—but"—she gulped—"but why? I mean, I d—didn't d—do anything. I mean, I j—just—"

"We have a couple of questions we want to ask your boyfriend. We want you where we can see you. And incidentally, the back is covered. So don't get dressed and decide to leave. What's your name?"

"It—it's Gretchen."

"All right, Gretchen. Get dressed. Underwear will do."

"B—but I— All I've got is panties. I mean, that's all I ever wear. I—"

"Just pick something you can't hide a gun in," I snapped, "and then get out of that bed. We came here to talk to Clark, not to you. Is that clear?"

"Y—" She swallowed. "Yessir."

"All right, Gretchen. Move it."

I returned to the living room, and sat on the zebra-striped couch. I'd left the bedroom door ajar, and I could hear the squeak of bedsprings. Turning to Clark, I said coldly, "This is Thursday, Arnold. Thursday afternoon. Right?"

His lips twitched in an insolent smile, but his con's eyes revealed nothing. "If you say so, man."

"Do you remember what you were doing Tuesday?"

"Tuesday?" He frowned elaborately. "Any special time, on Tuesday?"

"Let's start with noon. Where were you at noon Tuesday, Arnold?"

"Well, ah—" Mockingly coy, he shifted his gaze toward the bedroom. "Well, Tuesday, about noon, I was right here. See, I'm taking a few days off from work to take care of this bad back I got, and I need a little, ah, help. So I—"

"Gretchen was with you. Is that what you're saying?"

"Oh, come on now, man. You ain't *really* interested in Gretchen, are you? Or"—he leered—"or *are* you? Because if you are, maybe I could—"

"Listen, Arnold—" I allowed a moment of menacing silence to pass. "The word I get is that you're smart—con smart, street smart. So you know as well as I do that unless you and Gretchen can produce a marriage license, your parole is kaput. Finished. Right this second. If I want you back inside, all I have to do is make a call to your parole officer. That's all—just one call."

He made no reply. But his entire body had become rigid. His powerful muscles were jungle-tense.

"Have you got that, Arnold? Do you understand where we're at, you and I?"

His lips twisted behind the close-cropped beard. "Yeah, man. I know where we're at. But then I knew that a long, long time ago."

"Okay, Arnold. Good. We're making progress. Now—" The bedroom door was opening. Dressed in tight-fitting faded Levis and a ribbed red sweater, Gretchen stood in the doorway. Her body was breath-taking. She wasn't concealing a thing.

I pointed to a low, sprawling ottoman. "Sit there, Gretchen.

120

Listen, but don't talk—not unless you're spoken to. Then answer. Have you got it?"

Nodding, she moved obediently to the ottoman. She looked like a wistful, chastened child who'd been told to sit in the corner. Her amethyst eyes sulked; her mouth was pursed in a pout.

I turned back to Clark. "As I was saying, Arnold, this situation is very, very simple, so far as you're concerned. If you answer all my questions—every one—then I might consider not busting you for parole violation. Repeat, *might*. Have you got that?"

"Yeah," he said. "I got that, all right." The black eyes were obsidian-hard. The muscles were bunched at the torso, corded at the neck and across the upper chest.

"All right, let's go through Tuesday, Arnold. What time did—" I caught myself and gestured for Markham to take Gretchen from the room. As he gripped her arm, he brushed her breast with the back of his hand. She drew sharply away from him. I waited for the click of the door latch, then I turned once more to the suspect. "What time did Gretchen leave on Tuesday?"

For a moment he didn't answer. Then, speaking with slow, deadly deliberation, he said, "She left about seven o'clock."

"In the evening?"

"Yeah."

"Where'd she go?"

"She went home."

"Where's home?"

"She lives with her folks." He smiled mockingly. "They live in Pacific Heights, as a matter of fact. With all the other rich folks."

I nodded, matching his mocking smile. "You do all right for yourself, Arnold. Your old friend Lieutenant Friedman says you're into the radical chic skam. It looks like you're making a pretty good thing of it."

"Yeah. Well, you know how it is. I mean, you got to keep up with the times."

"Is that how you met Marjorie King? On the radical chic circuit?"

Instantly, his expression changed. He was smiling now. His muscles were slackening. He was visibly relaxing—amused, apparently, at the mention of the woman's name. If he was acting, it was a masterful performance. But cons are good actors.

"So that's what it's all about," he said softly. "Some junkie sticks a blade in Marge's old man, and right away you figure it's me. Naturally. I mean, that'd be the best move in the world for me to make—the way you figure, anyhow. Marge and I have this thing going. She buys me a few knickknacks—" His hand circled the room. "So, right away, I figure that the smartest thing I can do is kill old Tom. I mean, it *figures*. It's the old doublethink shit. I mean, it'd be so stupid for me to kill him that no cop in his right mind would suspect me of killing him. So I kill him. Naturally. And Marge and I live happily ever after, down here in the quaint, picturesque Fillmore. We—"

"King was killed with your knife, Arnold."

"With *my* knife?" The idea seemed to delight him. Lapsing into the broad, cackle-hooting, thigh-thumping patois of the ghetto, he crowed, "Why, man, you got to be *jiving* me. Why, shit, man, I ain't used a blade for—lessee—ten years, give or take a year or two. I mean, you go 'round flashing them blades, the first thing you know there's this other dude. And he got a blade, too. And the fustest thing you know, him and you is a-starting to—"

"The knife has your prints on it, Arnold. Two nice, clear prints. And a man answering your description was seen leaving the scene of the crime. Now"—I raised two fingers—"now, that's two strikes, Arnold. Two quick strikes. Let's forget that you're a parole violator. I don't need that, to put you away. I've got enough, right now, to book you on suspicion of Murder One. So"—again I paused—"so if I were you, Arnold, I'd try to come up with a pretty good alibi for your whereabouts on Tuesday from, say, eight to midnight. Because if you can't come up with something pretty good"—I spread my hands—"well, I'm afraid I'm just going to have to take you downtown, Arnold."

As I'd been speaking, I'd watched the muscles once more tighten

122

beneath his satin-brown skin. Suddenly he was sweating. He'd come forward in the chair, tensed. His legs were braced beneath him, ready. His hands were tightly clenched. I shifted my body so as to bring my hand closer to my revolver. If he came for me, I'd throw myself backward on the couch, kick him in the gut with both feet, and draw my gun as I rolled off the couch and up to face him, crouched over my revolver.

He spoke in a low, choked voice. "I been inside for nine years, man. Nine out of the last ten years. I went in when I was twenty-seven, and I'm thirty-six now. A few years, and I'll be forty years old. And I'm telling you—*warning* you—that I'm *never* going back. I mean—" With enormous effort, he unclenched his right hand, raising a trembling forefinger to point at my torso, dead center. "I mean, I'm warning you," he whispered. "I'm not going back. Every con who gets out of prison says he'll never go back. And most of them *do* go back—quick. But I'm not just *saying* it. I'm *telling* you: I am *never* going back inside, no matter *what*. I don't know who it'll be—you, right now, or some other cop somewhere else. But somebody'll have to kill me. I'll push it until he does. I'll push it all the way—all the way to hell. But"—he drew a long, chest-heaving breath—"but I'm not going back."

Looking into those black eyes, feeling the full force of his gut-gathered ferocity, I believed him. I'd heard the boast made countless times in the past: "You'll never take me alive." But the first sight of a gun—the first crack of a shot—could cancel countless streetcorner vows.

Yet I believed Arnold Clark. Because at that moment, I knew that he was capable of hurling himself across the room at me, his fingers clawing for my throat. And I knew that only a bullet could stop him.

But if I believed his threat, could I also believe that he'd killed Thomas King? He had a good thing going with Marjorie King. Would Clark have risked his freedom to get more? It didn't seem like a smart move. And Clark was smart.

"We're up to seven P.M. Tuesday, Arnold," I said quietly. "What happened then?"

He was making a visible effort to control himself. I could gauge the intensity of the struggle, watching his bared muscles. Finally: "*Nothing* happened then," he said. "Not one goddamn thing. I stayed home. All night. I didn't see nobody all night. Nobody at all."

"How about phone calls?"

For the first time, he faltered. "I got one call. From—Marge."

"What time was that?"

"About nine, I guess."

"Was she phoning from home?"

"I guesso." He frowned, then shrugged. "Yeah. Sure."

"What'd you talk about, Arnold?"

"Well, hell. I mean, we just talked, you know?"

"A little sweet talk. Is that it?"

His lips twisted. "Yeah. Right. A little sweet talk. What's the matter? Does that bug you?"

"That you're making it with white women, you mean? Is that the question?"

"That's the question, all right."

"Then the answer is no, Arnold. It doesn't bug me at all. From what I saw of Marjorie King, I can't say that I particularly like her. So I don't really give a goddamn whether she gets herself screwed up with someone like you. Is that plain enough?"

He didn't answer. The black fire in his eyes still smoldered.

"How long did you talk?"

He shrugged. "A half-hour, maybe."

"So you'd finished talking about nine thirty."

"About that, yeah."

"What time did you go to bed?"

"About ten thirty."

"How often do you talk to Mrs. King? Once a day?"

"Yeah."

"Have you talked to her today?"

"No, man, not today. I mean"—his eyes slid toward the back bedroom—"I mean, it's still early. You know? Don't push me."

"Did you talk to Mrs. King yesterday?"

He frowned, then said carefully, "Yeah, as a matter of fact, I did."

"What time?"

"Oh"—he shrugged—"sometime in the afternoon, I guess." He was idly fingering his pagan necklace.

"Did she mention that her husband was missing?"

"No."

"What was the conversation about?"

Again he shrugged, but now his lips parted in a sly, knowing smile. "It was the usual. She likes me to tell her how it was going to be next time we get together. She likes to hear what I've got planned. You know—a little advance publicity, you might say." He was caressing the largest tooth strung on the necklaces: a small curved tusk, ivory-white.

"What kind of things did you plan, Arnold?"

"Oh, come on, now. I mean, you're already giving me all that jive about how I'm a big-ass lawbreaker, and everything. You can't expect me to—"

"Answer the question, Arnold. I've already got all I need if I want to put you back inside. The rest is just trimming, and you know it. On the other hand, if you help me, you help yourself."

"Yeah. Well"—he lazily shrugged—"well, I guess you'd say Marge is a little kinky. Like, she goes for the rough stuff, you know? That's what most white chicks want. They want to be cuffed around a little, you know?"

"Does Marge like whips?"

"No, man. She's not on that trip. And if she was, I wouldn't go along. I mean, a little rough stuff, that's cool. If it turns on the white chicks to get cuffed a little, it makes a lot of black guys feel good to oblige. It's called relieving aggressions, you know?"

"That's how you fell for rape, eh? Relieving your aggressions on white women."

The obsidian eyes were expressionless. He still fingered the single small ivory tusk.

"How about the husband, Arnold? Mr. King? Was he kinky, too?"

"Well, I never met the dude. But according to Marge, he was a real swinger. I remember her telling me, one time, how they got into the swapping scene. According to her, it was all his idea."

"According to her."

He shrugged.

"How often do you see Mrs. King?"

"Oh—" He shifted in the chair, elaborately relaxing—preening, rippling his bulging stud's muscles. "Oh, once a week, I guess. Sometimes twice a week. It depends."

I looked around the apartment. "Did Mrs. King give you the money for this?"

The response came ghetto-quick: "Did she say she did?"

"I'm asking you, Arnold."

"Then the answer is no. Not for everything, anyhow."

"Where d'you work? When your back isn't bothering you."

"I work at Gamble's tire-recapping plant."

"How much do you make a week?"

"Wal, now—" He lapsed into his broad, black man's drawl. "Wal, I make about eight-five dollars a week. 'Course if I wasn't a cullud man, and wasn't on parole, now, I 'spect I'd make cornsiderably more. Like, twice as much, cornsidering that I just about kill myself, recapping those mother-loving little ole tires. But"—he spread his huge hands—"but that's how it is. You don't hear *me* complaining. No sir*ee*. Not me. I jus' takes what they give me, and smile when the boss-man pockets the difference. Because I—"

"How do you account for the fact that your knife was used to murder Thomas King?"

"I *don't* account for it," he answered. "Because I don't believe it. And the reason I don't believe it is because it's not true."

"Your prints were on the knife, Arnold."

"Yeah, well, you *tell* me that. And, naturally, I'm not calling you

126

a liar. I mean, you're a cop, and all—a *po*-liceman. But you know as well as I do, Lieutenant, boss, that unless there's a full set of prints on that knife, then all you got is a little ole hunch. I mean, unless you got a full set, you don't have any evidence. Right?"

I allowed a moment of silence to pass as I stared directly into his eyes. "Let's put it this way, Arnold," I said softly. "Let's just say that I've got a problem that you can help me with. The knife. And then let's say that *you've* got a problem that I can help *you* with. Your freedom. Now"—I looked at him with bogus solicitude —"now does that help clarify things for you?"

"Sure. And I'll be *glad* to help you, man." His facetiousness perfectly matched my own. "Except that—" He broke off, seemingly struck by a sudden thought—or playing the role of surprised innocence to perfection. "Hey," he said slowly. "Hey, maybe I *can* help you."

"Good."

"Does that knife have a black handle? Is it a switchblade?"

I didn't allow my expression to change. "I'm asking the questions, Arnold. Remember?"

"Yeah. Well, if it has a black handle—a smooth black handle with silver bolsters, then it could be mine, all right. Except that it was stolen from me—two, three months ago."

"Tell me about it, Arnold. Tell me all about it. Everything."

"There's nothing to tell. Not really. I mean, I came home one night, and my place was all tore up. I mean, there were pictures pulled down and furniture slashed and everything. And my bedroom—my bureau and everything—man, it was a real mess. Whoever did it, they were mostly after my clothes. I mean, they ripped up my clothes like you wouldn't believe. But the funny thing was, practically the only thing that was missing was my knife—that switchblade. I figured he'd used it to do the ripping, and then took it."

"Who's he?"

"Well—" He hesitated, measuring me with a shrewd sidelong glance. "Well, I always figured it was Bruce King."

"Why?"

"Well, Marge and I, we'd been—you know—seeing each other for quite a while, and the kid found out. And he's kind of a creepy kid, anyhow. Fact is, the way he found out about us, he was following his mother. He—"

"How do you *know* he followed her?"

"Well, Christ, I got the word that he was hanging around outside. I mean, in this neighborhood, it's a wonder he didn't get himself in some real hot water, hanging around. But anyhow, I heard about it. And Marge, I guess she cooled him. But my place was messed up just a little while after she cooled him. So I always figured it was him."

"Did you report this vandalism?"

He looked at me. "To the police, you mean?" It was an incredulous question.

I regarded him thoughtfully, then said, "Let's say, for the moment, that you're telling the truth. Let's say Bruce King took your knife. And let's just say, for the sake of argument, that he used the knife to stab his own father. That's a little hard to swallow, of course. But let's assume that's what happened. Now"—I paused, compelling his attention—"now, if that's really what happened, then how is it that Bruce King's fingerprints aren't on the knife? How is it, in fact, that your prints are the only ones on the knife?"

"Man, don't ask me. I mean, you're the detective."

"You're not being very helpful, Arnold."

He didn't answer.

"However"—I looked him over, taking my time—"however, Arnold, I'm going to go along with you, to the extent of at least checking out your story. I'm going to leave Sergeant Markham here while I pay a call on Mrs. King. You know why Sergeant Markham's going to stay here, don't you?"

"I imagine it's so I can't phone Marge."

I nodded. "Very good, Arnold. Now, before I leave, there's one last point. If you have any aluminum oxide or powdered

128

magnesium around the premises, I'd like to know about it. You might be able to help yourself if you can show me either one."

"How can I help myself?"

I waggled a finger at him as I rose to my feet. "Ah, ah, Arnold. You're asking questions again. All I want from you are answers. Remember?"

"Yeah. Well"—he shifted suddenly in the black leather chair—"well, I don't know anything about any—whatever it is."

"Aluminum oxide. And powdered magnesium—like they use to make fire bombs. You aren't planning to fire-bomb anything, are you, Arnold?"

He shook his head.

"No, I guess you wouldn't, Arnold. You've got a pretty good thing going with white girls, it seems to me. There's a little risk, of course. But nothing like bombing things. By the way, does Gretchen slip you a little money once in a while?"

He taunted me with a slow smile. "Once in a while. I mean, I give her what she needs. Why can't *she* come across with a little something once in a while? You know—share the wealth. Like, her folks are loaded. So what's the harm?"

"Does Gretchen like you to play rough, too?"

His taunting smile widened. He began stroking his stomach. "Gretchen is different," he said softly. "She's for fun—*my* fun. Marge, that's different. After all, like I said, I got to keep my aggressions relieved."

"You seem very fond of your aggressions."

He was still smiling. "Shit, man, I didn't even know I *had* any aggressions until some psychiatrist at 'Q' told me about them. I just thought I was doing what comes naturally."

"You were, Arnold. You were."

Seventeen

I used a call box to contact Friedman, reporting on the Clark interrogation and asking him to arrange for a twenty-four-hour stake-out of Clark's apartment.

"So you do figure Clark as a suspect," he said.

"Well, he admits to owning the murder weapon. And he was involved with the dead man's wife. They could be planning to collect the insurance and live happily ever after."

"Do you think it's possible Bruce King could have framed Clark?"

"Do you?"

"I asked you first," he said.

"Anything's possible, I suppose. While Markham and Sigler are keeping an eye on Clark, I've got Culligan checking out Clark's neighbors for confirmation that Clark was really vandalized two months ago."

"I can't quite see the kid premeditating his father's murder, and framing it so that only Clark's fingerprints appeared on the knife. Still—" Friedman paused, speculatively.

"What is it?"

"I don't think I mentioned it this morning," he said, "but the lab says that Clark's fingerprints were normal. Just plain fingerprints, on the grip and the bolsters of the knife. But a lot of the knife had blood on it—the blade and part of the handle."

"So what's the point?"

"The point," Friedman said thoughtfully, "is that you'd think the fingerprints would have been in blood."

"Hmm." I frowned at the call box.

"Did Clark have any explanation for the aluminum oxide and the powdered magnesium?"

"No."

"I wonder if Bruce has a chemistry set left over from childhood," he mused.

"I'll let you know. I'm on my way to the King house right now. Where's Canelli?"

"He got back from Pacifica about a half-hour ago."

"Does he have anything to report?"

"Not really. As usual, we'll have to wait for the various scientists, so-called, to submit their findings. However, to me it seems pretty obvious that Winship was shot Tuesday night. Maybe he saw the murder in progress."

"Or maybe he saw the murderer, but didn't know it."

"That could be," he agreed. "Because if he was trying to escape from a bad guy, he picked a strange destination. As opposed to the nearest police station, for instance. He set himself up, really. By the way, I got a report from the bartender at The Shed. He says that Winship left immediately after Diane Farley left, Tuesday night. Which means that since he was driving and Diane was walking, Winship could've gotten to her apartment before she did. Not much before, probably—but enough. He could have murdered King, and left. Or he could have seen the murder committed, and left. Then Diane could have arrived on the scene."

"Are you going to get corroboration that Winship left right after Diane left?"

"Naturally. And I'm still trying to find out what clothes Diane was wearing Tuesday night."

I checked my watch. The time was almost four o'clock. "I'd better be going. Send Canelli out to the King residence, will you? I'll meet him in front."

"Roger. From the sound of it, assuming you don't decide to arrest mother and son on the spot, I think we'd better stake out the King house, too."

"Yes."

"Maybe I'll give Canelli the job. He seems a little puffed up after his starring role down in Pacifica. There's nothing like an all-night stakeout in February to instill a little humility in the ranks. We don't want Canelli to get ideas above his station. I mean, Markham's bad enough, without Canelli getting into the act."

"I couldn't agree more. Tell Canelli to hurry, will you? Markham and Culligan are stuck at Clark's until they hear from me."

"Will do. Good luck."

"Thanks."

As Marjorie King sat down on a small Queen Anne love seat, she folded her hands calmly in her lap. Her knees were pressed primly together. Her mouth was set in a thin, disapproving line. Plainly, I was annoying her. Watching her—remembering the things Clark had said—I tried to visualize the black man abusing her as they lay naked together.

I deliberately led her the long way around, teasing her with fleeting references to Arnold Clark, watching her squirm. Finally, hopelessly trapped, she admitted the affair. She had no choice. But even then she clung to her cold, disdainful poise.

"How'd you find out about Arnold and me?" she asked.

I let her squirm for a last long, sadistic moment. Then I said, "We discovered that you were picked up together at Emile Zeda's. Technically, you have a police record. You—"

"A lot of people got picked up that night."

"How many times did you and Clark go to Zeda's?"

"Twice. And what's wrong with that, anyhow? Zeda's a—a showman. He's harmless. A harmless charlatan."

I nodded. "That's true, Mrs. King. As you say, a lot of people got picked up that night. But there's another problem, where Arnold Clark's concerned."

"He's a parolee, you mean. Which gives you the license to persecute him. He hasn't—"

"No, it's not that," I said quietly. "It's more serious." I paused, fruitlessly trying to disconcert her. Then I said, "Your husband was killed with Arnold Clark's knife."

Her lips curled. "Really?"

"Yes, Mrs. King. Really. Clark admitted owning the knife. When you talk to him, he'll tell you." I paused again, then said, "What'd you do, Mrs. King—call Clark at nine o'clock Tuesday, and tell him where he could find your husband? Is that how it went?"

"No, Lieutenant. That's not how it went." Her voice was even, her eyes steady.

"Do you deny being intimate with Arnold Clark?"

"I don't deny anything. I don't admit anything, either. I think it's time I called my lawyer."

I nodded quick agreement, gesturing to the hallway and the phone. "By all means, call him, Mrs. King. But be sure you tell him the whole story. It's very unwise, you know, to keep anything from your lawyer. For instance, you should tell him that Arnold Clark's fingerprints are on the knife. You should also tell him that neither you nor Arnold Clark have alibis for the time when your husband was murdered. And then you should—"

"I was home that night," she flared. "With my son. You—you can ask him."

I smiled at her. "I *will* ask him, Mrs. King. As a matter of fact, there are several things I want to ask him—several things that Inspector Canelli is asking him right now."

"Wh—what sort of things? What're you talking about? Are you trying to insinuate that—"

"First," I cut in, "I want to ask Bruce about a report that he was so upset over your affair with Arnold Clark that he actually followed you down to Hayes Street, spying on you. Then I want to—"

"That's a goddamn lie." Suddenly her lean, elegant face was

a death's head of malevolence: pale flesh drawn taut over a stark skull shape, eyes blazing in sunken sockets. Her mouth was open, revealing small, clenched teeth.

"It's not a lie, Mrs. King," I said softly. "It's not a lie, and you know it. You also know that your son, out of spite, actually vandalized Arnold Clark's apartment. And you—"

"You're accusing me of murder, Lieutenant." She was breathing hard now. Her fists were furiously clenched. Her eyes still blazed.

"You didn't tell me the truth, Mrs. King. Not the whole truth. So now I'm wondering what else you didn't tell us. I'm wondering whether—"

"Get out," she hissed. "You've got no right here. You—you've got no right to—"

I rose to face her. "Speaking of rights," I said quietly, "I want to give you yours." I drew the plastic card from my pocket and began reading. With my first words, she suddenly whirled, rushing into the hallway. As I finished speaking, she was furiously riffling through a small morocco book of phone numbers. When Canelli and I left the house, she was speaking vehemently to her lawyer.

"Boy, oh, boy." Canelli ruefully shook his head. "That Mrs. King is really something. I mean, she's one tough cookie."

I pointed ahead. "Pull around the corner, there. I don't want her to think we're hanging around. Park so you can see her house in the mirror."

"Lieutenant Friedman said I was supposed to stake her out. He's sending me someone to cover the back, I guess."

"Yes."

"Are you going to have a show-up for Clark?" He pulled to the curb and switched off the engine.

"Not until tomorrow. I've got him staked out. I want to see whether he'll jump for us. And the apartment next door to his is empty. With a little help we can hear him talking on the phone."

"Oh." Round-eyed, he nodded solemnly. "A little help" meant

electronic eavesdropping—inadmissible as evidence, but useful. Learning of occasional departmental illegalities, Canelli invariably managed to appear primly surprised.

"How'd you come out with Bruce?" I asked.

"Well, of course, I didn't lean on him too heavy, because he's a minor, and everything." Canelli looked at me for approval. I nodded. "But naturally," he continued, returning his gaze to the rear-view mirror, "naturally, I asked him whether he'd ever tailed his mother down to the Fillmore."

"What'd he say?"

"He denied it—*really* denied it. Which makes me figure that maybe he really did. Tail her, I mean. One thing is for sure: he's a real unhappy, real screwed-up kid. I don't think either one of his parents give a damn what happens to him. They buy him everything he wants, and give him plenty of money to spend, and then they just forget about him. It's like they say: poor little rich kid." Canelli shook his head.

"Do you think he vandalized Clark's apartment?"

"Well, to tell you the truth, Lieutenant, I didn't get around to that. I mean, the first thing I knew, the mother was giving us the old heave-ho. So I didn't—*Hey!* There's the kid now, coming out of the house."

Twisting in the seat, I saw the boy striding rapidly toward our corner. He wore a corduroy car-length coat, sneakers and the standard teen-ager's faded blue jeans. He walked with his hands in his pockets, shoulders hunched, head lowered. He was a tall, gangling boy, and moved with a loose, tangle-limbed stride. He was walking on our side of the street; he'd pass beside us.

I put my hand on the door handle. "I'm going to talk to him. It's five o'clock—it'll be dark in an hour. You'd better set up the stakeout. I'll get a ride home in a squad car. If anything develops, call me at home. Got it?"

"Yessir."

With the boy less than twenty feet away, I opened the door and stepped out on the sidewalk, facing him.

135

"Hello, Bruce."

Startled, he pulled up short. His pale, harried eyes darted involuntarily aside, as if he were seeking escape.

"Can I talk to you for a few minutes?"

"I"—he gulped—"I . . ." He couldn't finish. His eyes still seemed to seek escape. Canelli had started the car and was moving away. Bruce King and I were standing alone on the sidewalk. I saw him shiver, digging his hands deeper into his pockets. Yet for February the evening was warm. We stood in a pale rectangle of winter sunlight, framed by the shadows of two tall luxury apartment buildings.

"Where were you going?" I asked.

"I was just—just going for a walk."

I gestured to a nearby cement wall. We could lean against the low wall, talking, and still share the sunlight. Obediently, he followed me. We stood side by side, facing the sidewalk, not looking at each other. It was a good situation in which to interrogate a shy, skittish subject.

"I wanted to talk to you before we left. But . . ." I let it go unfinished.

"But you got my mother mad." He said it wearily—resigned to his mother's cold, purposeful anger.

"Do you know what she was mad about?" I asked.

When he didn't reply, I glanced at him. In profile, his sallow, pimple-blotched face was almost grotesque. His nose was too large, his chin too small. His cheeks were sunken, as if he were wracked with sickness. His lips were too full and too red, incongruous contradictions in the prematurely ravaged face. His pale, uncertain eyes were moist, as if he were perpetually on the point of tears. He blinked constantly and often swallowed spasmodically. Glancing quickly down the length of his thin frame, imagining him stripped, I realized that his body, like his face and neck, was thin and pallid. His thin blond hair clung to his skull in lank, formless wisps.

"Do you know what's bothering your mother?" I pressed.

136

He licked his rosebud lips. "She—I think she—she thinks that you—" He gulped. Then in a miserable rush: "She thinks that you —you blame her for my—my father's murder."

Turning my eyes away from him, I nodded. "Yes," I answered. "Yes, she does."

I could feel him painfully gathering himself. Finally, hesitantly, he asked, "*Do* you blame her?"

Still with my eyes averted, I answered, "I don't know what to think, Bruce. I've got a job to do. I've got to do it, no matter who it hurts."

"She didn't kill him. She hated him. He hated her. But she wouldn't kill him." Now his voice was strangely disembodied. His moist eyes were blinking, glazed by shock and grief.

"I wasn't accusing her directly, Bruce. But we have—certain information that makes us think she might've *had* him killed."

"Her boyfriend, you mean. The black man." His voice was still hushed.

"Yes. That's right." I paused, then said, "You knew about your mother's—friendship with Arnold Clark."

"Is that his name?"

"Yes."

He didn't respond. It wasn't necessary.

"Did you also know about your father's—friendship with Diane Farley?"

At the question, his body suddenly stiffened. "I didn't know *her* name, either," he whispered. "I didn't know *any* of their names. I—I might've known, once. But I forgot. Sometimes I forget my parents' name. I can't stand the sound that their names make, inside myself. Or my own name, either. Sometimes I can't stand the sound of my own name. I—" He choked, half sobbing.

I had to finish the job. "Arnold Clark says that you ransacked his apartment a couple of months ago, Bruce. He says that you tore it up—ripped up his things, just out of spite. Is that true?"

His mouth was working impotently; he couldn't speak.

"Nothing was taken," I said quietly. "There won't be any

137

charges pressed. I guarantee that. It's just that I have to know. I have to know whether Arnold Clark is lying to me, or whether he's telling the truth."

"He's lying." Now the boy's voice was totally uninflected—dead. He was drained.

"What about Diane Farley, Bruce? Were you ever inside her apartment?"

"No. Never." He said it in the same dull, dead voice.

"Did you leave your home Tuesday night? For any reason?" Now, finally, I turned to stare at him directly. I saw his mouth twist into a wry, exhausted smile. Tears streaked his cheeks.

"No, Lieutenant. I didn't leave the house Tuesday night. Not for any reason. No reason whatever, so help me God."

"You say that very"—I hesitated—"very fervently. I wasn't asking you to swear to it. All I need is a simple answer."

He pushed himself away from the wall. The effort seemed enormous. "I'll swear to it, Lieutenant. I'll swear to anything. Just name it. I'll swear to it." And without a word, he turned toward the corner, walking with his slack, shambling shuffle. He was heading toward home. I decided to walk in the opposite direction.

Eighteen

I stripped off my shirt, then slipped the handcuffs and holster from my belt. I placed both the gun and the cuffs in my dresser drawer, together with the belt clip of ten extra cartridges and my shield case. I slipped off my trousers, then stepped to the full-length bedroom mirror and gazed for a long, critical moment at the small roll of loose flesh above the beltline of my shorts. In the past half year, had the roll increased? Were the pectoral muscles sagging, the thigh muscles softening? Half turning, I allowed my abdominal muscles to go loose. In profile, there was an undeniable belly bulge. My muscle tone was gone. But it was late, nine thirty. And in fact my weight was within ten pounds of my best proball years. I was only forty-three. I still had most of my hair. I could still . . .

The phone rang.

Was it news from a stakeout? Canelli, at the King house? Markham, at Arnold Clark's? I strode quickly into the living room.

"It's Ann, Frank."

"Hi. I tried to call you."

"We just got home. We've been shopping. Both the boys lost their wool ski socks. Do you know how much ski socks cost?"

"Yes. I used to buy them, too, remember?"

"Do your children ski?"

"Of course. It was part of their mother's Junior League image. Indispensable. Skiing, and tennis lessons."

139

"We both have ex-spouses with social pretensions. I never thought about it. Do you think it's significant?"

"I hope not."

I could hear her giggle. "You have a certain talent for one-liners, Lieutenant. Deadpan one-liners. Do you know that?"

"I'm glad you think so. Will you have dinner with me tomorrow night?"

She hesitated. Then: "Can't you get away for the weekend?"

I sighed. "I'm not sure. This case—the film maker—isn't going very well. I can't ask my men to put in extra hours while I'm out of town for the weekend."

"Doesn't Pete owe you some time?"

"Not really. Anyhow, we don't keep books. Besides, this case is mine. Pete has his own caseload."

"Maybe you'll get lucky."

"Maybe. We've got a few things developing. It's a matter of how they work out. Why don't we plan on dinner and the evening? The *whole* evening. Let's play it by ear. If I get a break with the case, we can just throw some things in a suitcase, and take off."

"The next time a policeman takes out after one of my children," she said, "I'm not going to become emotionally involved. Do you think I'd've liked you better as a professional football player?"

"No."

"Why not?"

"Well, in the first place, I wasn't really a very successful football player."

"You probably lacked the killer instinct."

"You may be right. Anyhow, I'm glad I didn't know you then. It was a very tense period in my life. Plus I was married."

"Did you ever have any affairs when you were married?"

"Yes, toward the end. But they didn't mean anything. By that time, I was a so-called P.R. man at my father-in-law's factory. Which meant that, in addition to drinking with important clients and driving them to the airport, I was also expected to provide them with girls. Which meant that I—fouled up, once in a while.

140

But by that time everything was ending—my marriage and everything else."

There was a silence. Then, in a small, chastened voice, she said, "You never told me any of that, darling. Not really."

"I know." I paused, then said, "Sometimes things—come easier, over the phone."

"It must have been humiliating. I mean"—she hesitated—"having to provide girls. You must have felt . . ." She let it go unfinished.

"Yes. That's how I felt."

I heard her draw a deep, pensive breath. Then she said, "That's a terrible time—the end of a marriage. It took me a long time to realize it. A long time after the marriage was over, I mean."

I didn't reply, and a small silence began to lengthen. Suddenly there was no more to say—not over the phone. Ann felt it too, and we quickly said good night.

I'd no sooner broken the connection than the phone rang again.

"This is Canelli, Lieutenant."

"What's doing?" I sat down in an easy chair, crossing my bare legs.

"Well, I turned up something pretty interesting," he said. "So I thought I should call you, like you told me."

I sighed softly. Canelli rambled, especially on the phone. Looking down at my legs, I saw goose flesh beginning.

"I wasn't disturbing anything, was I, Lieutenant? I mean, you said that I should—"

"No. It's fine, Canelli. What've you got?"

"Well, about quarter to eight," he said portentously, "Mrs. King got her car, and she went out. So I followed her. So what does she do, for God's sake, but she drives out Sacramento Street —to the thirty-six-hundred block. And she parks the car and goes up to this old Victorian house that's all dark, except for a couple of lights in the back of the house. So she starts beating on a door knocker, hard. She knocks for a minute, maybe, but nobody answers. So she tries the door, and when that doesn't work, she acts like she's real pissed off. So finally she opens up her purse and gets out a paper and writes on it. She slips the paper in the mail slot of the door, and she turns around and leaves—gets back in her car, and drives off, back home. So, naturally"—he paused for breath—"so naturally, I took down the address of the house, and I checked it out. And guess what, Lieutenant?"

I sighed again, recrossing my legs. "I give up, Canelli. What?"

"Well, the house belongs to Emile Zeda. You know—that guy with the Satan cult, or whatever they call it."

"I'll be damned."

"Yeah. I mean, here she is, the night before her husband's funeral and everything, knocking on Emile Zeda's door."

"Did you follow her home?"

"Sure."

"Did she go right home?"

"She sure did. I mean, she didn't have anything else on her mind, except going to Zeda's place. I could tell by the way she was acting."

"Where are you now?"

"I'm phoning from a bar. I mean, I didn't know whether you wanted me to stake out Zeda's place or anything. So I thought I'd better call you at home, like you told me."

I took a moment to consider, then said, "You may as well get some sleep, Canelli. We've got four men out on stakeout on this case already. I don't want to authorize any more overtime. Not now, anyhow."

"Yeah, I see what you mean, Lieutenant. I don't blame you."

"Why don't you pick me up tomorrow morning about nine? We'll stop by and see Emile Zeda on our way to the office."

"Roger. Good night, Lieutenant."

Nineteen

"There it is." Canelli pointed. "That big old Victorian, there. That's Zeda's. Jeeze, it looks like a haunted house, or something. I bet it hasn't been painted for fifty years. Except for the door." He pointed. "I mean, that's a red, red door."

"Blood-red, no doubt. Come on—let's see what he says."

The front door opened on the third stroke of a huge dragon's head brass knocker. We were greeted by a pale, slightly built young man with the eyes of a zealot and the voice of a sleepwalker.

"Is Emile Zeda in?" I showed him the shield. "I'm Lieutenant Frank Hastings. This is Inspector Canelli."

"Yessir, he's in." The young man hesitated, plainly considering asking us to wait on the porch. When I stepped forward, he gave way.

"What's your name?" I asked, watching the youth struggle to swing the heavy door closed.

"Hawley. Leonard Hawley."

"Do you work for Mr. Zeda?"

"Yessir. I've worked for Zeda five and a half years." His soft servant's voice was touched with quiet satisfaction. Looking at him more closely, I realized that he was older than I'd first thought. Thirty, perhaps.

"How many other employees does Zeda have?"

"Just me. I'm the only one who's always here. The others— come and go."

"Do you mean that you help him with his—Satan worshiping? Or just with the house?"

"I help him with everything." He said it as if he were pronouncing a benediction.

"But mostly with his services, or whatever you call them."

"We call them revels." He pushed back his shoulder-length hair with a quick flick of his wrist. The gesture's nervous vitality contradicted Hawley's soft voice and diffident manner. Studying the glittering intensity of his eyes, the formless softness of his mouth, and the limb-locked stiffness of his movements, I decided that Leonard Hawley was a creature of contrasts, rigidly suppressed. Dressed in a kind of rough peasant's jerkin, shapeless trousers and open sandals, Hawley was perfectly suited to the vaulted Victorian gloom of the hallway.

For a moment we stared at each other. Then impassively he turned away, murmuring that he would bring Zeda to us.

I turned slowly, surveying the spacious foyer. To my left, a broad baroque staircase led majestically upward—only to stop at a blank wall. The staircase had been partitioned off at the first landing. To my right, a double archway was draped in heavy black velvet curtains. The archway opened on a large drawing room, doubtless reserved for Zeda's "revels." Only two other doors remained, one beneath the stairs, another leading to the rear of the house.

"Hey, Lieutenant," Canelli whispered. "Look at that."

Following the jerk of his pudgy chin, I saw a human skull displayed in a carved niche set into the hallway's rich wooden paneling. Perched on the skull was a black raven. Beside the skull was a wax-incrusted candleholder.

"Jeeze, I thought it was real," Canelli breathed. "The bird, I mean."

"Shades of Edgar Allan Poe."

"Have you ever been here before?"

"No." I looked around. "Maybe I've been missing something."

"Yeah, me too. I think I'll bring Gracie here some night. She's very big on all that astrology and occult stuff and everything. She'd love all this crap."

I pointed to a carved wooden music rack which displayed a black-bordered placard announcing Friday night revels at eight o'clock. "Tonight's your chance, Canelli."

"Hey. Yeah. Jeeze, maybe I will."

"You can put in for extra hours. Surveillance."

As he looked at me doubtfully, the small below-stairs door opened. The low doorway was filled with Emile Zeda.

He wore a white toga gathered at the waist with a thick black cord. His waist was slim, his chest deep and powerful. His head was shaved, his thick mustache and beard were trimmed to a sharpened Satan-shape. His thick black eyebrows completed the demonic illusion, arching high over bright, wild eyes. An angry scar traversed his forehead, angling upward from eyebrow to skull-crown.

Zeda was approximately six feet tall, weighed about two hundred, and was probably about forty years old. As he advanced on us, I noticed that he wore tennis shoes.

"I was downstairs, jogging in place," he said. "Thus the tennis shoes." He looked from one of us to the other. "Which of you is Lieutenant Hastings?" His voice was a deep, theatrical bass. As he spoke, I caught the gleam of two gold teeth.

Before I could reply, he raised a peremptory hand, palm forward. He fixed his sorcerer's eyes on me. "You. You're Lieutenant Hastings." It was a showman's statement, not a question. Without waiting for a reply, he turned toward the rear door. "We'll talk in private, gentlemen." He led the way down the back hallway to a small library lined floor to ceiling with books. Over his shoulder, Zeda ordered Canelli to close the library door. Zeda sat behind a huge, claw-footed table, imperiously gesturing us to twin chairs, which could have come from the hall of a medieval castle.

As I sat down, I caught Canelli's eye. His awed expression almost made me laugh.

"Well, Lieutenant, what can I do for you? What is it this time? Another hand-wringing complaint from the ASPCA?" As he folded his arms across his barrel chest, I noticed that Zeda wore his fingernails almost an inch long.

"No, Mr. Zeda. The ASPCA isn't my beat. I'm with the Homicide Detail."

"Call me Zeda," he said brusquely. "Just Zeda." Plainly, he equated the single name with some special, extrahuman attribute.

"All right." I cleared my throat.

Unfolding his arms, he began to drum his long, gleaming fingernails impatiently on the arm of his chair. Our roles, I realized, had become inexplicably reversed. He was acting the inquisitor's part.

I started again. "We're investigating the death of Thomas King. You probably read about the case in the papers."

"I never read the papers. However, I know that he was killed. Tuesday night, wasn't it?"

"Yes. Tuesday. How'd you learn about it?"

"From Mrs. King. His wife. She's a follower of mine."

"When did she tell you about the murder?"

"She didn't *tell* me about it, Lieutenant." His voice was elaborately patient. "She *wrote* me about it."

I decided to pretend innocence. I wasn't yet ready to reveal my knowledge of Mrs. King's visit. "She wrote you about it?" I asked.

"Yes, I have no phone. No radio. And no TV, of course."

"And you don't read the newspapers."

He condescendingly nodded. "That's correct. For my purposes, it's best that I receive information and impressions directly, either by word of mouth or handwritten letter. I can't afford to submit my mind to electronic debasement."

"When did Mrs. King write you?"

"I received the note yesterday, along with several others. Yesterday evening, about ten o'clock. Very often, my followers drop

146

notes to me during the day. I read them between ten and eleven at night. During the week, I select a few of these notes, on which I comment during our Friday night revels. Leonard collects the notes and puts them there." He gestured to a shallow brass tray.

"What's the nature of these notes?"

Zeda shrugged. "Experiences. Impressions. Thoughts. Anything, really. You'd be amazed, the things I get."

"You must have a lot of very devoted followers."

"Well"—he permitted himself a smile—"I don't know whether 'devoted' is quite the right word."

"Sorry," I answered dryly. "Fanatical, then."

"Much more apropos, Lieutenant." He studied me for a long, sardonic moment, then said, "You should come to one of our revels, Lieutenant. For someone in your, ah, profession, I think it would be a valuable experience. Come tonight. I'll see that there's a place for you."

"Thanks. Maybe I will."

"Bring a friend." Plainly, he meant a woman. Thinking of Zeda's troubles with the vice squad, and imagining Ann beside me in his audience, I smiled faintly. Then casually I asked, "Do you still have Mrs. King's note? The one she dropped off last night?"

"No. Every morning, without fail, my followers' notes are burned."

"Do you burn them?"

"Leonard does."

"What did Mrs. King's note say?"

"Simply that her husband had been murdered. It was a simple reaching out—a desire to communicate her loss."

"Will Mrs. King be coming to your service tonight?"

"I don't know."

"Does she come every week?"

"No. She only comes once a month, I'd say. She's a very independent-minded woman. Very strong-willed."

"I know. And I'm surprised that she'd be involved in—your kind of thing. She doesn't strike me as a cult worshiper. And as a matter of fact, she doesn't strike me as someone who would feel she had to come out last night just to 'reach out.' "

"Why not, Lieutenant?" It was a quiet, probing question—a psychiatrist's question.

I shrugged. "It's just a hunch—a feeling. But in my business, you learn to trust your feelings."

"It's the same in all businesses, Lieutenant. The conscious mind is incredibly complex. And the subconscious is more complex still —a complexity compounding a complexity. The human subconscious is nature's crowning achievement. And feelings, intuition, are a tracery of the subconscious. Anyone who can listen to his feelings learns a lot."

"I agree. By the way, did you know Thomas King?"

"No, I never met him. But by coincidence I knew both his wife and his business associate. So I felt—" He paused. "I felt close to Thomas King. I felt as if I knew him."

"His business associate?"

"Charles Mallory."

"Mallory is one of your followers?"

"Not really. He's only come twice to revels. Both times with friends. He should have come more often. Mallory is a homosexual. He would have profited immensely."

"How so?"

"Our sect is aberrant. Oddball, to coin a phrase. People who are also aberrant find a great meaning with us. A *great* meaning." Accenting the last phrase, he fixed me with a meaningful stare.

"What's there about Mrs. King that's aberrant?"

"She lives a dual life," he answered promptly. "Most of us do, of course—at least in fantasy. But she feels the conflict more than most. On the one hand, she's an utterly straight wife and mother. And most important, she's an executrix. A very good executrix, I'm told. All of which means that really she has very strong drives to dominate and excel. Which is an expression of her primitive side. And Marjorie's primitive side is at once stronger than most, and at the same time more rigidly suppressed, especially by the demands of her career. Which produces conflicts. And these conflicts draw her to me, because the worship of Satan—the *bacchanalian* worship of Satan—is the essence of primitive behavior. It's a release—the ultimate vicarious release. And that's precisely Marjorie's problem: finding a suitable release for her primitive emotions. So I help her."

I smiled. "Some, uh, nonbelievers say that members of your flock could release just as many of their inhibitions by going to a porno movie, and maybe smoking a little pot at the same time."

His answering smile mocked me. "There are doubters everywhere. It's easy to doubt. To believe—that's difficult."

"Is Mrs. King's affair with Arnold Clark an example of her primitive instincts finding release?"

He inclined his shaven head. "Precisely." He showed no surprise.

"Are you acquainted with Arnold Clark?"

"Certainly. He was one of those who had an unfortunate experience with your centurions."

"How would you describe Clark?"

His eyes shone with pleasure; his forked devil's beard parted to reveal teeth clenched behind false-smiling lips. "Clark is a magnificent specimen—a perfect example of the species American primitive, subspecies ghetto black. He's exactly what Marjorie King needs."

"I think Clark is a conniving, sadistic bastard. His kind is the same, black or white."

"From your point of view, Lieutenant, he's precisely that."

I nodded, glancing at Canelli. It was his cue to ask a few questions while I tried to sort it all out. Canelli came to attention in his chair.

"I got to go along with the lieutenant," he said. "Mrs. King just doesn't strike me as the type who'd have to get herself comforted by 'reaching out to you' or whatever you call it. I mean, she's just too tough. Smart and tough. I just don't see her trotting out at night and leaving notes for you to ease her mind or something. Not only that, but she told the lieutenant, just yesterday, that she didn't think you were all that much. So it seems to me that"—Canelli paused for breath—"it seems to me that we've got a contradiction here. I mean, we've got her telling us one thing, then acting like she believes something else about you—at least, to hear you tell it."

Zeda had been listening with an air of amused tolerance. Now he said, "What was your name again, Inspector?"

"It's Canelli."

"Certainly." He nodded, mockingly ceremonious. "Well, Canelli, I'm afraid you'll have to quiz Mrs. King on that point. I'd have no idea, of course, what she told your lieutenant concerning her opinion of me. But, meanwhile, I think you should reflect on the nature of our sect. Better yet"—he turned to me—"better yet, you should come to one of our gatherings. Ventilate the mind."

I rose to my feet. Canelli did likewise.

"I might just do that, Zeda, as I said. Meanwhile, though, we have to be going." I turned to the door. Then, pretending a sudden afterthought, I turned back to face him. "I wonder whether you'd mind getting Leonard for a minute."

"Certainly." Also on his feet, he touched a button on his desk. Almost immediately Leonard appeared. He stood serflike in the doorway, hands slack at his sides, mutely staring round-eyed at Zeda.

"Have you burned the messages you received yesterday, Leonard?" I asked.

His eyes didn't leave Zeda, who was standing just behind me and to my left. Leonard hesitated, then nodded his head, obviously on cue. "Yessir, I burned them." He turned his blank gaze on me, nodding woodenly.

I turned immediately to Zeda. "I'd like to see the messages you've received today, Zeda."

He shook his head. "No, Lieutenant, I can't show them to you. Of course, you can get a court order. But short of that, you can't see them. If I showed them to you, I'd be striking at the corner-stone of our edifice."

"If you put me to that trouble, Zeda, you'll be giving yourself some trouble, too. Most people in your position violate a few municipal codes. Usually there's no problem. But there *can* be problems. Do you understand?"

He accepted the threat with a monk's arm-folded stoicism, eyes half closed, head slightly bowed. It was a masterful performance. "I've put up with persecution for years, Lieutenant. It never stops. But neither do we. The worship of Satan's darkness is the one message this neohedonistic American society can't bear—because it can't bear the truth. But our message comes through. Because it's the truth."

I turned on my heel and walked to the doorway. "I'll be seeing you, Zeda. Maybe you need a little persecution to keep you on your toes. After all, look what it did for Christ."

We left the house to the echo of Zeda's mocking laughter.

Twenty

"If I were you," Friedman said, "I'd go to Zeda's prayer meeting tonight."

"Why?"

"Well, for one thing, you could find out whether Zeda's parishioners really do drop him notes in the night. Somehow that sounds a little fishy to me. Maybe Zeda concocted a three-ring, on-the-spot snow job to explain Mrs. King's visit. Besides"—he waved an unlit cigar—"besides, nothing else on this case is going anywhere. Diane Farley's clothing tested negative, and it turns out it's the same clothing she wore to The Shed. San Mateo can't give us anything on Winship's murder. Arnold Clark didn't do a thing last night except go to a double feature and then right home. He didn't even make a phone call, according to our illegal listening device. Mrs. King's lawyer has been in touch, and it'll take a Supreme Court order for us to search the King house for bloodstains. Even Charles Mallory didn't do anything last night but go home. Of course, his roommate, so-called, got back last night." Friedman leered. "That's where we should've had our bug—in Mallory's bedroom."

"Why'd you stake out Mallory?"

"Two reasons. First, Mallory profits by King's death, so it's just a percentage play. But also—" His voice lifted to a lightly bantering note. I knew what was coming. He'd turned up some-thing. "Also, Record's brand-new computer threw up Mallory's name, slick as a whistle."

"That gay bar thing?"

"Not the gay bar thing. Something a little heavier—and some-thing that, coincidentally, concerns your friend Zeda—which is another reason you should stay with him. Zeda, I mean." Fried-man consulted a few scrawled notes. "It seems that, three years ago, Charles Mallory had a live-in lover named Vance Gosset. And it seems that Gosset was a big fan of Zeda's. In fact, Gosset and Charles Mallory used to go to Zeda's prayer meetings."

"I know that. In fact—" I paused thoughtfully. "In fact, Zeda mentioned it. And, at the time, it seemed as though he was drag-ging in Mallory's name gratuitously."

Friedman nodded. "I wouldn't be surprised. He was pre-empting you, probably—just like he maybe preempted you on Mrs. King's note-passing. Anyhow, what happened, Gosset and Mallory went to a gay party, and got gassed—or stoned—and then proceeded to have a lover's quarrel. Mallory apparently made a pass at a hairdresser, and Gosset took exception. So to get even, Gosset flounced off home and climbed into Mallory's bed—they had twin beds—and Gosset shot himself in the left temple, after leaving a note that accused Mallory of being his 'murderer.' Which, apparently, Mallory wasn't, since he was off with the hair-dresser at the time of Gosset's death. But—"

"Jesus," I said, "I don't remember any of this."

"That's because it wasn't our case. It was listed as a suicide. And three years ago, the General Works Detail was handling sui-cides. Remember?"

"Oh. Right. Was Mallory charged with anything?"

"No. He got a lawyer, right away. Everything was cool."

I nodded.

"But here's the snapper." Friedman paused, plainly for the ef-fect. "The snapper is that Gosset's suicide note mentioned Zeda." Friedman again consulted his notebook. "Zeda was to 'preside over the transportation of his body to the next astral plane.' Which in plain language meant that Zeda presided over his funeral, which was apparently quite a black magic show—and which Mallory didn't like one little bit."

"This Zeda is into everything."

"Right. He's a real smart cookie. I did a little checking on him after I heard about Mrs. King's expedition last night. And I discovered that Zeda has several con games going, just barely inside the law. Apparently, in San Francisco, Zeda's only number two in this Satan cultist skam. A character named Sanda is number one. So Zeda has to try harder. And in fact Sanda brought suit against Zeda a couple of years ago, to get Zeda to trim his beard so it wouldn't look so much like Sanda's—who, of course, had trimmed his beard to look like the Devil's. So—" He paused for breath.

"What kind of con games is Zeda into?" I asked.

"The usual cultist skam. Getting his believers to endow his 'cause' with their worldly goods, once they shuffle off to the next astral plane. But even with all his little sidelines, Zeda is always short of cash, apparently. His bank account is overdrawn about half the time, and he's got a third mortgage on his house, which is about to be foreclosed. So—" Friedman tossed the notes aside, stretching his thick arms over his head as he leaned back in his chair, arching his beefy back. "So go to the prayer meeting. Get to know your friendly charlatan better. Take Ann. Have a few laughs."

I snorted ruefully.

"What's the matter?"

"We were hoping to get away for the weekend. Ann's kids are going skiing. So instead we end up at a side show for Satan freaks. Incidentally, Zeda calls them revels, not prayer meetings."

"So go away for the weekend. I'll look after the shop."

"No." I shook my head. "Thanks, Pete, but I can't. It wouldn't be right."

"Crap."

I shrugged. I was thinking of the weekend I'd shared with Ann in Big Sur. Was I being foolish? Should I . . .

"If I were you," Friedman said, "I'd marry the girl. She's got a good figure, and a good sense of humor—quiet, but nice and bright. Which complements your sense of humor—quiet, but mostly black. And she's got class, too. Which is the most important consideration of all."

"I know. But—" Again I shrugged.

"How long've you been divorced, anyhow?"

"Almost ten years. I was divorced a year before I joined the force."

"Well," Friedman said judiciously, "I think it's about time you quit feeling sorry for yourself and rejoined the fray. Get married, in other words. I've had my eye on you for some years now, and I've come to the conclusion that—"

"Listen, Pete, this isn't exactly the time to—"

"I've come to the conclusion," he continued smoothly, "that you need the love of a good woman, plus you could profit by some of the hassles that the rest of us endure, raising kids."

As I shifted sharply in my chair, his expression changed. Putting up a restraining hand, he said seriously, "No, don't pop off. Hear me out, then pop off. After all, like I said, I've given this matter long and careful thought over the years, and I think I've finally got you figured out. So therefore, if I don't let you in on it, all that effort's gone for nothing. Right?"

"Wrong. No one asked you to—"

"It all started, the way I figure it, when you were, say, fourteen or fifteen. I figure you as one of those high school types that types like myself spent a lot of time envying. You were good-looking, amiable and smart—without being too smart. Plus you were well-coordinated, plus you had just enough bottled-up aggressions to make you a good knock-'em-down football player, thanks to your father leaving your mother in the lurch, no doubt. So anyhow"—he drew a deep breath—"so anyhow, you came up a winner, all through high school and college. Everything fell into place. You even made it to the pros, after college. Right on schedule. But then you made the mistake of marrying an heiress, which meant that you were a society football player, which is a contradiction in terms. Unlike, say, a society gynecologist, for instance. So pretty soon both your marriage and your career began to go on the rocks. So you got out, which was a good move. But you—"

"Listen. I've really got to—"

"Wait. I'm almost finished. Getting out, like I said, was a good move. There was no way in the world you could stay in Detroit. But unfortunately you left your two kids behind. And that's the problem. Those kids. Because it's obvious that you're very fond of them, whether you talk much about it or not. Which is why I say that if you married someone like Ann, who's got a family already, you'd be back in business as a parent. Now, the way I see it, your kids are— How old's your girl?"

I realized that I was glowering at him. But grudgingly I said, "She's seventeen."

"Yeah. And your boy's a little younger. Right?"

"Fifteen."

"Right. Well, the way I see it, your kids are going to get sick of the country-club scene. They may even get a little sick of their mother. If you remember, the last time your kids were out here, you all came over to our house for a barbecue. And I had the strong feeling that your kids were very turned on at the idea of maybe living in San Francisco. But they realize that you aren't equipped to handle them, either in your apartment or your head. So"—he spread his hands—"so marry Ann, and you might all live happily ever after."

As I stared at him, I realized that my outraged sense of invaded privacy had unaccountably passed, leaving me the helpless victim of a sudden rush of memories. Friedman had been right. Early in the game, I'd been a graceful winner. But late in the game, I'd come up a loser—a failure. He hadn't spoken of the drinking problem I'd had even after I'd joined the force. At thirty-three, I'd been the oldest rookie at the police academy. Every night, I'd gone home to my bottle and my maudlin memories. Friedman knew about the drinking. But he hadn't spoken of it. So he'd debased his own analysis. He'd . . .

Friedman's phone was ringing. I heard him answer, and I knew it was Clara, his wife.

"Just a second, honey." He covered the receiver and looked me full in the face. For once, his eyes were wholly serious. "No hard feelings?"

I got to my feet, shaking my head as I met his gaze. "No hard feelings."

"Good." Immediately his face lapsed into its habitual expression of ironic inscrutability. "In that case, I'll talk with my wife, who's getting up a bridge game tonight. Are you going to Zeda's?"

"Why not?"

"Exactly. Why not? If you want me, I'll be home playing bridge and drinking beer."

Twenty-one

The nearest parking place was a half-block from Zeda's house, on the opposite side of the street. As we walked the half-block, I automatically glanced around, wary of muggers. The slums were a scant five blocks away. Zeda's affluent clients would be tempting victims.

With the exception of a dim light in the entryway, the decaying house seemed deserted. All the windows were dark. Yet as we drew closer, I saw faint light escaping from the heavily draped front-room windows—the room that lay beyond the velvet-curtained archway.

"It looks like a Halloween party," I said.

"Will they let us in?" Ann took my arm and pulled me close. "It's almost eight thirty. We're late."

"Don't worry. I was invited. By the master himself."

"This is a wonderful idea, darling. I've been curious about Zeda for months, especially since I read that article in the *Sentinel* on occultism. Did you read it?"

"No."

"Well, it's a big thing, you know. Satan worshiping. Witchcraft. The black arts. It's all part of America's obsession with the occult. And the *Sentinel* gave a lot of space to Emile Zeda, and even had a picture of him. He looked exactly like Mephistopheles."

"Big deal." I lifted the dragon's head knocker and let it fall. The blood-red door was opened by a girl wearing a long black gown, cut very low. Her dark hair fell almost to her waist. Her face and shoulders were chalky white; her eyes were deeply shadowed. Standing in the gloom of the candlelit foyer, she looked like a character from a late-late horror movie.

The girl skillfully negotiated a ten-dollar "contribution" from me without raising her voice above a sepulchral whisper—and without blinking. Then as she ushered us to the archway and ceremoniously parted the black velvet curtain, she whispered that the revel would only last another twenty minutes.

We found seats in the last of six rows of folding chairs. A quick head count put the audience at thirty-two, with several empty chairs. At five dollars a head, Zeda's gross for the week was only a hundred and sixty dollars.

Zeda had changed his white toga for a long black robe with a red Satan's head emblazoned across the chest. He stood on a low, black-draped stage that filled the far end of the huge room. Behind Zeda was a catafalque, also draped in black. A girl lay on the catafalque. Dressed in a chiffon-sheer gown, she lay motionless, in perfect profile. Her long blond hair fell almost to the floor. Her eyes were closed. As she breathed, her breasts rose and fell in a slow, subdued rhythm. The scene was lit by the pale light-cone of a single spotlight, set in the ceiling. Two braziers were placed at either end of the catafalque, each filled with a guttering circle of orange and yellow flames dancing above a pool of scented oil. Behind the girl, dressed in a studded headsman's jerkin and black leather hood, a medieval figure stood with arms impassively crossed. The executioner held a huge curved scimitar in one hand, a cat-o'-nine-tails in the other. But somehow the menacing image of a hulking headsman was flawed. The oiled muscles were stringy. The neck was scrawny. The thigh-length jerkin revealed frail, knobby-kneed legs. And then I recognized Leonard Hawley. The single spotlight clearly caught the zealot's glitter in Leonard's eyes. A muscle was quivering spasmodically in Leonard's shoulder. He'd been holding the same position too long.

Zeda was speaking slowly and compellingly, in a low, resonant voice. "We see hypocrisy all around us," he was saying. "We see sin, but we realize that others can't see it—*won't* see it. *Refuse* to see it. It is we who can recognize the face of temptation, because we are followers of the master of temptation. And this is why we are persecuted. Because we know of secret rites and rituals, we are feared. We know the dark side of the soul. We realize that the priest must have his bottle, the pastor his libertine. We know it because we do not condemn it. Therefore, we are privy to the black secrets of all the ages. We seek out these secrets —embrace them—yes, practice them. Because we realize that only in hedonism can truth be found. Others go to church on Sunday, and to pornographic films a day later. Contemporary man is therefore unclean—because he denies hedonism. He conceals it, blames it on his brother. And so each time he embraces Satan, he poisons his psyche with guilt. Therefore we say that to embrace Satan is to cleanse ourselves of the poison of hypocrisy and guilt. To preach the passion of Satan, therefore, is to cleanse society. So let us probe within ourselves for our most primitive instincts, and make of them a ceremony. Let us purge ourselves—release ourselves. And let us invite others to our revels—so that soon our revels will no longer be secret, but will be shared with all."

As Zeda bowed his head over the last solemn words, a low murmur of anticipation passed through the audience. Chairs squeaked surreptitiously as bodies moved unconsciously forward. The overhead spotlight was dimming as Zeda turned with slow, grave ceremony to the catafalque. Leonard was stepping back—one step, two steps, three. Zeda was in Leonard's place, just behind the gauze-draped girl. With the spotlight dark, the brazier flames revealed only the pale shape of the girl and the demonic face of Zeda, suspended above the iridescent red-embroidered Satan's head. Everything else was black—deep, velvet black. I felt Ann's fingers slowly tightening on my arm.

160

Long Way Down

As Zeda began speaking, I saw his hands rising slowly: to disembodied claw shapes, just above the girl's pale body.

"Tonight," Zeda intoned, "our sister Gail has come to us for awakening. She has been prepared. She is ready. She has learned Satan's sacraments, she has studied the teachings of hedonism. And so—tonight—she has placed herself before you, that she may share with you the affirmation she makes. For as she acknowledges my touch, she accepts Satan, promising herself to the eternal mysteries of darkness and delight."

As he spoke, the shape of the claw hands changed as they hovered delicately just above the girl's body, forming themselves to the contours of her torso. Now Zeda raised his head slowly up toward the ceiling. His lips were parted; the two gold teeth caught the faint light of the braziers. His scar was outlined in jagged, angry shadow. His eyes were closed. The girl's eyes, too, were closed. As the tempo of her breathing quickened, her breasts rapidly rose and fell.

Zeda touched the girl, one hand on her breast, the other hand just above the pubis. At the touch, her body arched in a sudden, sensuous spasm. As he began to caress her, the urgency of her response quickened. Her body and his hands moved together, swelling to a wild, abandoned rhythm. Then, deliberately, Zeda slowly lifted his hands until they were once more suspended just above the girl's passion-arched body. As if she were responding to the urging of invisible wires, the girl began to rise with Zeda's hands. Her eyes were still closed; her lips were drawn back from tight-clenched teeth. Slowly, somnambulantly, she was sitting up, swinging her legs to the floor on the far side of the catafalque. Now she sat on the edge of the catafalque, facing Zeda. Her back was to the audience, her arms were braced wide. Then as Zeda's hands returned to her body, she slowly rose to stand before him, motionless. Her head was thrown back. The gauze of her gown clung to her straining thighs. For a moment, the erotic tableau was frozen. Zeda towered above the girl. From behind the two figures, a third shape emerged. It was Leonard, moving to one of the two

161

braziers. As he passed a hand over the brazier, the low, lingering orange flame sprang suddenly into bright crimson. At the same moment, Zeda's hands began to move. His fingers crept up the girl's arms, finding her shoulders. Then, gripping the gossamer gown, he drew it down—first to her waist, then over the swell of her flanks, finally allowing the gown to fall from his hands, disdainfully. In the fading light of the crimson flame, the girl moved to Zeda, lifting her arms to embrace him. As Zeda stood motionless, head raised haughtily, hands once more at his sides, the girl pressed her pale body against the black silk robe. Her flanks began to move rhythmically. As the red light flickered out, she writhed with one last, frenzied thrusting, then shuddered, satiated. As she slumped, Zeda raised his right arm to support her. Her torso arched back across his arm, inert. Her blond hair fell straight down over pink-crested breasts. Now Zeda moved his left arm behind her knees, lifting the limp body, holding it displayed, just above the black-on-black catafalque.

At that instant, the second brazier erupted with a sudden flare of white light, blinding bright, limning the girl's body with a harsh, obscene brilliance.

Leonard had slipped behind the second brazier, scattering his magic powder into the guttering orange flames.

Only magnesium could produce that quick, blinding glare. Aluminum oxide had probably accounted for the crimson flame.

As the audience gasped, then began to murmur, I turned to Ann. "Let's go."

"Go?" she whispered incredulously.

"Yes. Now. Right now."

"But—"

"Come on, Ann. This is business. I want to get out of here while the lights are still down." I got to my feet and walked to the black velvet curtain, parting it for Ann. The foyer was deserted; the girl with the ghoulish eyes had disappeared. I opened the heavy front door, waited for Ann, and finally closed the door behind us. I took

162

her arm, turning her toward my car, parked at the end of the block.

"What *is* it, Frank?" she demanded. "What's wrong?"

"I don't have time to explain," I answered, gripping her arm and hurrying her along, "but you're going to have to help me." At the car, I opened the passenger's door. A frown was gathering between Ann's eyes as she turned toward me. Her small chin was stubbornly set.

I drew a deep, exasperated sigh. "I told you this was partly business, tonight," I said sharply, "and now it turns out that Zeda is a murder suspect. I don't have time now to explain it to you. But I want you to do exactly as I say. And I don't want to argue with you about it. Now—" I pointed to the car's interior. "I want you to get in there and lock yourself in. I've got to find a phone, quick. I'm going to call in for assistance. It'll take me five minutes. Maybe ten. While I'm gone, I want you to keep track of how many people come out of Zeda's. I want you to count them. *Carefully.* Is that clear?"

I saw her swallow. Contritely, she nodded.

"All right. Now, as I say, I won't be gone for more than ten minutes, at the outside. And, while I'm gone, there won't be any danger to you—*none.* Otherwise, I wouldn't leave you. But, just to be safe, I want to make this clear: You *aren't* to leave the car. You aren't to unlock the doors or roll down the windows. Now, do you understand?"

"Y—" She swallowed again. "Yes." Then, with pixy-lit eyes, she said, "Yes, *sir.*"

"Come on, get in the car." I gripped her arm, intending to push her inside. But instead I drew her quickly to me, kissing her lightly on the forehead, then shoving her inside. As I straightened, I heard the door lock click.

"If anyone bothers you," I said through the window, "blow the horn. Don't open the door. Just blow the horn."

She nodded.

The thirty-six-hundred block of Sacramento was a polyglot neighborhood, residential and commercial. Some of the stores were on the way up, some on the way down. The houses followed the same pattern. All the buildings were attached, each sharing a common wall with its neighbor. At nine o'clock, the only lighted sign I could see nearby was a bar, a block and a half away. Walking as fast as I could, I covered the distance in less than a minute. The small tavern was jammed with a noisy neighborhood crowd, celebrating Friday night. A bleary-eyed man was propped inside the single phone booth, gesturing broadly as he talked. I turned to the crowded bar, impatiently waiting for the bartender to look in my direction. I caught his eye, beckoned to him, and showed him the shield, asking for his phone. Reluctantly, he motioned me behind the bar, setting the telephone on a water-pooled drain counter, half covered with inverted glasses. I dialed Communications, and was put through to Homicide. But Friday night was taking its usual toll: we'd had two barroom knifings and a streetcorner shooting. Only Sigler was on duty, catching the calls.

"Want me to round up a crew?" he asked.

"Where's Lieutenant Friedman?"

"He's at home. He—" Sigler hesitated. "He's playing bridge."

"I'll call him. Keep your line clear until you hear back from Friedman."

"Yessir."

I broke the connection and dialed Friedman's home. As I listened to the phone ringing, I checked the time. Seven minutes had elapsed.

"Hello?" It was Pete's voice.

In thirty seconds, speaking in a low voice, I explained the situation. "I've got Ann in the car, watching the front door," I finished. "I've got to get back."

"I'll send you a crew. What'd you want?"

"Three inspectors and two black-and-white backup units. Tell the black-and-white units to park at either end of the thirty-six-hundred block of Sacramento Street, lights out. Zeda's house is in the center of the block. Tell the inspectors to meet me at"—I hesitated, thinking of Ann—"at my car, I guess. I'm at the east end of the block."

"Roger. Do you want me to come out?"

"No. But stand by. And call Sigler. He's catching."

"Okay. Good luck."

"Thanks." I nodded to the hard-eyed bartender, and walked outside. On the sidewalk I paused momentarily, fearful that a patron of the bar might have overheard my conversation and would follow me, rubbernecking. A single rubbernecker miraculously attracts a dozen. But no one came out. As I walked toward my car, I checked the time again. Twelve minutes had passed. The street was almost deserted. The neighborhood was marginal. A woman alone in a car was taking a risk.

As I passed Zeda's house, I saw his front door open. Three members of his audience came out, all well dressed. The girl with the ghoulish eyes was closing the blood-red door behind the trio. Chatting quietly, the two men and one woman turned toward me, walking slowly. I passed them with eyes averted, making for my car, parked at the far end of the block. Ann was seated on the passenger's side. In the half darkness, her eyes were wide.

"Those three make twenty-nine," she whispered timidly.

"Good." I looked at her, smiling suddenly. Whispering playfully, I hissed, "You don't have to whisper. We've got 'em cornered now."

"Well," she said primly, "the way you were manhandling me, I didn't know *what* was happening."

Still smiling, I turned my gaze toward the still-darkened house. "Maybe I can get you one of those medals for civilian heroism. If you can think of some way to butter me up, that is."

"What'd you have in mind?"

"I'll let you know. Maybe you can—"

Again Zeda's door opened. Two women came out, both middle-aged.

"There's one more left," I said. "There were thirty-two spectators, all together."

"Frank, what's *happening?* What's it all about?"

"I'll tell you later. Not now. All you've got to do is follow instructions. It'll all be over in a few minutes. With luck."

At that moment, a black-and-white car turned into the block, proceeding slowly. I rolled down my window, and surreptitiously nodded as the two patrolmen passed. I didn't recognize them, but they knew me. In the mirror, I watched them swing a U-turn in the next block, so that they could park facing Zeda's house. They switched off their lights. As the second black-and-white car cruised by, heading for our end of the block, I saw the last member of Zeda's audience leave. With luck, only four people remained inside: Zeda, Leonard, the girl with the ghoulish eyes and the girl on the catafalque. As the second car took up its position directly across the street from us, I turned to Ann.

"All you have to do is stay here," I said. "Just sit tight, like you did just now. There's absolutely no danger. None at all. You're safer right here, with that squad car, than you'd be anywhere else in the city. But to make certain nothing goes wrong, I want you to lock the door and keep the windows up. Clear?"

"Yes." She nodded impatiently. "I will. I promise. But it's not fair for you not to tell me what's—"

"We're going to take Zeda and the headsman into custody." With my gaze on the blood-red door, I spoke brusquely over my shoulder. "That's all—repeat, *all*—that I'm going to tell you, at least for now. If there aren't any hitches, we can still have a nightcap, maybe."

As I spoke, Canelli's decrepit Ford station wagon turned into the block. I motioned for him to park, then come to our car. Seeing Ann, he grinned, transparently surprised and pleased. Canelli liked Ann.

"Hi," he said, slipping in beside her.

"Hi," she said.

He looked across at me. "What's doing, Lieutenant?"

"I'll tell you in a minute." I pointed ahead. A cruiser with two

166

figures was pulling to a stop just ahead of us. "There's the last two men. Come on, Canelli. Let's get in the back seat of the cruiser."

"Oh. Right." He clambered hastily to the sidewalk, smiled a last shy smile at Ann, and went to the unmarked car.

I followed him into the rear seat. I recognized Vasconcelles, from Bunco, but not his partner, who was introduced as Greer. As I continued to watch the red door, I quickly outlined the situation, carefully explaining that I was acting on suspicion, not proof. Felons weren't involved—or as far as we knew, guns.

"Still," I said, "there's a possibility we've got a murderer in there, so don't take any chances. But I don't think we want to go busting in with shotguns." I looked inquiringly at Vasconcelles, who nodded in judicious agreement. Vasconcelles was almost ready for retirement. His judgment was sound.

"Okay," I said. "Canelli and I will take the front. We know the layout. You two take the back." I consulted my watch. "We'll wait two minutes."

Agreeing, the two Bunco men got out of the car and crossed the street, walking with affected nonchalance. By the time I'd gotten a Communications radio hookup with Friedman, checking in, the two minutes had passed. I motioned for Canelli to get out of the car.

Twenty-two

As the door opened, Canelli and I separated, unbuttoning our raincoats and jackets, easing our hands between the folds of clothing toward our guns.

The girl with the ghoulish eyes stood before us, frowning now.

"We'd like to see Zeda, please." I stepped forward.

"Sorry, the revel's over. Write a note."

I showed her my shield. "This is police business." I pointed to a baroque hallway chair. "Sit down. Stay put."

"Oh, Jesus Christ. Not again." She flounced to the chair, deeply aggrieved.

"Where's Zeda?" Canelli asked her.

She gestured irritably to the door leading back to the rear of the house. "He's probably already in bed. He's pretty pooped, you know, after one of these things." She frowned. "Pretty exhausted."

"Where's Leonard?"

Her eyes moved to the black velvet curtain. The curtain was closed.

"He's in there." Her voice was hushed. "But—" She decided not to finish it.

I turned to Canelli. "You go find Zeda. When you've got him, call in Vasconcelles and Greer. I'll wait for you here."

"Right." Canelli strode to the hallway door, opened it cautiously, and disappeared. The girl made as if to rise. I lifted a hand, shaking my head. Petulantly, she sank back, gnawing at her colorless lips. I moved along the foyer's wall until I could see the girl, the velvet-draped archway and the two hallway doors, one leading beneath the stairs, one leading to the back of the house. Now the foyer was brightly lit; the candles had been extinguished. I eyed the archway, debating whether to take Leonard immediately. Finally I decided to wait for reinforcements. During the revel, I'd fixed the ground-floor layout in my mind. I knew that Leonard only had two ways out of the front room: the velvet-draped archway or the bay windows. If he chose the windows, the back-up units would pick him up. Every house in the block was attached. He'd be trapped in the street, with nowhere to go.

As I stood in the silent hallway, with my concealed hand resting on my revolver, I thought of Ann, alone in the car. I should have told her to drive on—go home. I'd made a mistake. I'd involved a civilian beyond the point of absolute necessity. I'd often disciplined subordinates for less. Had I been unconsciously trying to impress her? Had I . . .

The velvet drapes were stirring. They parted a single, surreptitious inch, then slowly, furtively closed. I'd been discovered. I considered a moment, then stepped forward. We'd lost the advantage of surprise. There was no point in waiting.

I moved to the left side of the archway, then suddenly grasped the drapes, jerking them open. As I did, I drew my revolver.

Momentarily, I could see nothing but twin circles of orange flame at either end of the catafalque. The braziers were still burning. As I stepped slowly through the archway, allowing the curtains to swing together behind me, I saw the white chiffon figure of the girl, disembodied in the darkness. She was pressed against the far wall, behind the catafalque. Her body was rigid, fear-frozen. But it wasn't my presence that frightened her. The front of her dress was ripped down to the waist, hanging in shreds.

I stood for a moment trying unsuccessfully to discover the hiding headsman. Then, clearing my throat, I said, "All right, Leonard. Step forward, slow and easy. This is a gun, and I—"

A dark figure leaped suddenly onto the low stage. At the same instant, I saw the polished curve of the scimitar, lying on the catafalque. As Leonard's leather-gauntleted arm swept toward the scimitar, I crouched, raising my gun.

"Hold it right there, Leonard. *Hold it.*"

But he was in line with the girl now. I couldn't shoot. With the scimitar in his hand, he faced me, at bay. The light from one of the braziers caught his eyes, wild behind the headsman's mask. His lips were drawn back, teeth clenched.

"Drop it. I'll shoot."

Momentarily, all movement stopped. Except for the rasp of Leonard's breathing and the guttering of the braziers, all sound ceased. Then, muttering incoherently, he whirled toward the girl, swinging the sword high overhead. I raised my gun, aiming at his back. But I couldn't risk a shot. The girl screamed. It was an exhausted, whimpering sound, too soft to bring help.

Should I shoot at the ceiling, to sound the alarm?

No. A shot could bring the sword slashing down. I watched Leonard's hand grip the girl's long blond hair, saw him sling her slack body away from the wall. Now my only target was a masked face over the girl's bare shoulder. The scimitar glittered against the white gown. The girl was moaning. Her eyes were rolling up. Her body was going limp.

I spoke softly. "Drop the sword, Leonard. I've got eight officers here. There's no way out."

"There's a way out—right past you. I'm going out—out past you." His voice was a high, aggrieved falsetto.

"You can't, Leonard. You're trapped. Throw it down. Make it easy on yourself." I was still standing just inside the archway's velvet curtains. I braced my feet wide apart, setting myself behind my gun.

Yet I knew I couldn't fire. And I knew that I would retreat before the sword.

170

Long Way Down

With his fist knotted in the girl's hair, he jerked at her savagely, dragging her toward the catafalque. She was only half conscious; her legs wouldn't support her. If she fainted—went completely limp —he couldn't hold her. Then I could risk a shot. The range was about twenty feet. I'd be shooting at a shadow. But if she fell to the floor, I'd try it.

Directly behind the catafalque now, he quickly crouched down behind his victim, giving up his grip on her hair, as he circled her waist with his left arm. The girl sagged forward. Placing the sword on the catafalque, he used his right hand to cuff her cruelly in the face—once, twice.

"Stand up." His voice was low, furious. "If you don't stand up, I'll kill you. I swear to Christ, I'll kill you."

"You've already killed two men, Leonard," I said. "That's enough."

The headsman's hood revealed only his nose and mouth. I saw his lips writhing like wounded snakes.

"I didn't even know their names. But you'll kill me for it. Only Zeda knew. But you'll kill *me*." The last word, both a shriek and a whisper, reverberated in the darkness like the distant cry of a wounded animal.

"Zeda's being arrested right now," I said quietly. "And the woman, too. We'll arrest her. They did it for money, Leonard. King's money. They just used you. They're to blame, more than you. But this makes it worse, what you're doing."

"It *can't* get any worse. But it *does* get worse. It *always* gets worse. It never changes. *Never*." His voice dropped to a low, querulous note. He was talking to himself now, muttering. I saw the girl stir. In the faint light of the braziers, her half-open eyes stared at me dully.

"Put the sword down, Leonard. I promise you, we'll take care of Zeda. We'll—"

"I'm going. I"—he choked on a sudden sob—"I'm *going*. Get back." His puny muscles strained. Suddenly he screamed, "God-damn you, get *back!*" He snatched up the sword. He was half carrying his victim toward the far end of the catafalque. With her feet dragging, ankles limp, the girl was dead weight. But then, as they rounded the catafalque, she suddenly stiffened. Leonard lurched, thrown off balance by the girl's shifting weight. Instantly, the brazier toppled; fire spilled in a flaming yellow pool. Flame found the gauzy white dress. The girl screamed. The flame leaped to her waist, touched the long blond hair. She was falling to the floor, engulfed in flame. The figure of the headsman leaped across the flame-pool. He was charging me—a demon, straight out of hell. The sword caught the leaping light of the fire. I threw myself to my left, firing as I fell. The sword sliced the air above my head. I fired again. The velvet curtain ripped apart; the headsman-shape was momentarily silhouetted in the hallway light. Screams filled the room. I was on my feet, dodging around the blazing catafalque. I threw myself on the heavy window drapes, dragging them down. The girl's dress was charred black; the odor of burning hair and flesh mingled with the acrid smell of the smoke. She was on her knees, arms braced wide, struggling. She wasn't screaming now; she could only gurgle, deep in her throat. As I reached the girl, her scorched body suddenly fell heavily to the floor. Her feet touched the flaming pool of oil. I threw the drapes over her, rolled her free of the flames, beating at the smoldering drapes with my hands. Then I lifted her in my arms and carried her into the hallway. At that instant, the front door flew open. A uniformed man stumbled into the foyer, off balance. He carried a shotgun, momentarily aimed at me. His partner was close behind, with a revolver. I recognized the men who'd parked across from my car.

Involuntarily, I raised the girl in my arms, to shield my chest from a shotgun blast.

"Hold it," I was shouting. "I'm Hastings, for Christ's sake." As recognition flashed in their eyes, I lowered the girl to the floor. From behind me came the sound of a door opening. I whirled, drawing my gun. Canelli stood in the doorway, gripping his own revolver, trained on me. I turned back to the uniformed men. As I did, I realized that the ghoul-eyed girl had gone.

"Call the fire department. Then take her to Park Emergency—fast." I gestured to the bundle at my feet. The drapes had fallen away from a single foot. The black-charred flesh was split red across the instep, revealing the white bone. Stooping, I flicked the drapery away from her face. Some of the blond hair still clung to her blackened skull. The odor was sickening. The patrolman with the revolver reluctantly holstered the gun and reached down for the girl. His partner was already out the door, heading for his car's radio.

"Jesus, Lieutenant. You hurt?" It was Canelli's voice.

"No. Where's Zeda?"

"I couldn't find him." He glanced up at the broad entryway stairway, partitioned across the first landing. "There's some back stairs that go up to the second floor. And there's even an attic, I think. I was just going up when I heard your shot." He was looking at me fretfully, frowning and shaking his head. "Are you sure you're all right, Lieutenant? I mean, you look like you—"

"Where's Vasconcelles and Greer?"

"I yelled for them to come in."

"All right—" I pointed to the small door leading below stairs. It was the same door in which Zeda had materialized earlier in the day, dressed in his white toga. The door was ajar.

"Leonard's our boy," I said. "And he must've gone down there. Be careful—he's got a goddamn sword." As I said it, I glanced back over my shoulder at the black-curtained archway. Smoke was eddying beneath the velvet. I could hear the sound of flames. Canelli and I were alone in the foyer. The two uniformed men had left the front door open; I felt a draught of cold night air, sucked past me by the fire. As I closed the front door, I heard footsteps overhead. I threw my head upward, shouting at the ceiling: "Vasconcelles! Greer! Can you hear me?"

Had it been their footsteps I'd heard—or someone else's?

A voice, muffled, acknowledged.

"Get out of the house!" I yelled. "The place is on fire. Go out the back, and stay there. *Keep the back covered.*"

The same muffled voice answered. Immediately, I turned toward the below-stairs door, drawing my revolver.

"All right, Canelli. Let's go. But remember that sword. In close quarters, it's better than a goddamn gun. So watch yourself. I'll go first. You come next. And close the door behind you, because of the fire. Clear?"

"Yessir."

I opened the narrow door, and saw a small landing and a narrow flight of basement stairs leading down to the ground-floor garage. The staircase was dark. I cautiously descended the first three stairs, then held up, waiting for Canelli to close the door behind us. As the door closed, my throat suddenly went dry. Crowded together on a narrow, pitch-black staircase, clutching our small pistols, we were perfect targets for a sword-wielding maniac, charging up the stairs.

I moved my hand to the light switch.

"Here goes the lights."

Close behind me, Canelli breathed an acknowledgment. I could feel him gathering himself. Raising my revolver, I flicked the switch.

Nothing.

"Have you got a flashlight?" I asked.

"No, sir. I left it in the car."

I hesitated. Should we go back up the stairs, get outside? Should we wait for the fire to flush him out?

No.

He could attack the firemen, entering the building to fight the fire. Overhead, I heard the sound of soft, furtive footsteps. Was it Zeda?

I moved my mouth close to Canelli's ear. "You cover our rear. If that door opens behind us, it's up to you. I can't shoot past you."

I heard him swallow. "Yessir."

"Are you ready?"

"Yessir."

"All right. At the bottom of the stairs, I'll move to the right. You move to the left." I pointed to the pale shape of a service door's single glass panel, the basement's only source of light. The door led out to the front sidewalk. The basement was a long way down. "If we can't find him," I whispered, "or if it looks too sticky, we'll leave by that door."

"Yessir."

Step by step, revolver raised, I began descending the stairs. For the first time I became conscious of the smell of scorched cloth —and flesh.

Had I been burned? Or had the stench of the girl's burned flesh clung to me?

I was close to the floor now. I stopped on the last step, holding my breath, listening.

Nothing stirred.

From outside came the distant wail of a fire siren. Our time was running out.

In the dim light from the service door, I made out the shape of a large car. The rest of the space in the two-tandem garage was a ghostly jumble of cartons and packing cases. The suspect could be hiding anywhere. At close quarters, in the darkness, he could decapitate one of us before the other could get off a shot.

Or he could have already escaped. He could have slipped through the service door, eluding the single team of backup men remaining in the street outside. He could have gone out the back while Vasconcelles and Greer were inside the house.

I took the last step. With my feet on the level cement of the garage floor, I began moving slowly to my right, bending double as I passed beneath the pale oblong glass of the service door. Behind me, I heard Canelli's feet shuffling softly to his left, following orders. I was passing between the car and the garage door. Reaching the car's far side, I saw that on my side of the garage the wall was clear, with a three-foot aisle between the wall and the car—an old Buick. On my side, there was no place to hide.

But the opposite wall was piled high with cartons and cases, some of them wardrobe-size. Canelli had drawn the dangerous duty. I saw the shadow-shape of his thickset figure, crouching low, steadily advancing. Canelli could be a bumbler. But he wasn't afraid.

Outside, another fire siren joined the first. Our time was almost gone. We couldn't hold back the firemen.

I'd advanced to the car's right front fender, making certain that Leonard wasn't crouched behind the Buick's grill. Now I drew back against the wall. I slowly straightened from my crouch, raising my revolver. From that angle, I could cover Canelli. We could . . .

An alien shadow shifted; a growl grated low in a savage throat. Suddenly a towering pile of stacked cartons flew apart like a stack of building blocks kicked by an angry child. As I sprang forward, the topmost cases came toppling toward me. Canelli's .357 Magnum roared—once, twice. Both muzzle flashes revealed an instant's glimpse of bare flesh and black leather. The sword was flashing up, down. The boxes were tumbling around me in nightmare slow motion. Canelli screamed, firing once more. I was wildly clawing at a carton, straining, pulling it away. Canelli was down, jammed against the car. The figure of the headsman was momentarily silhouetted against the access door. I snapped two quick shots as the door flew open, splintered by one crashing slash of the sword. I caught a glimpse of a fire engine pulling to a stop.

I knelt over Canelli, panting. "Are you all right?"

For a moment, he could only nod, mutely opening and closing his mouth. "I think so," he finally gasped. "I—I think the bastard hit my gun with th—that goddamn sword. Jesus." Now he began to shake his head, staring down at the floor, eyes blank. "Jesus, where's my goddamn gun, anyhow?" In partial shock, he began to paw futilely at the floor.

"Stay put for a minute or two," I ordered. "Find the gun, but stay put. I'm going after him." I quickly rose, making for the door. I was outside. As I stood momentarily motionless, scanning the sidewalk up and down the block, I heard Ann shouting: "He's here—*here!*"

The huge shape of a fire engine blocked out my car. Firemen were swinging to the ground, trailing their bat-black raincoats. As I dodged around the still-moving fire engine, I heard Ann screaming. Two steps, and I was in the clear. I saw the sword flash up over my car, then crash down. Once. Twice. The driver's window was crystallized. Ann screamed again. Another sword-blow split the window, top to bottom. A leather gauntlet reached through the window halves, groping for the door handle. He wanted my car—and Ann. The car was more than a hundred feet away. It was an impossible shot with my short-barreled revolver. I was in the middle of the street, running hard. I couldn't . . .

From behind me, a shot cracked out. Leonard jerked upward, arms and legs flung wide. He was falling backward from the car. As I covered the last few yards, he hit the pavement, spread-eagled. He gasped and gurgled as blood streamed from his mouth, choking him, pooling on the pavement beside his head. His limbs jerked. His torso arched upward, straining in death's final spasm. His eyes were bulging, his neck was grotesquely corded.

Then, sighing softly, he fell back, dead. I jerked open the car door. Eyes wide, Ann simply stared, wordless. She was unhurt. I heard myself mumbling inarticulately, telling her again to stay in the car—keep quiet. Then I turned away, advancing on the towering old Victorian house. Flames were bright in the bay window now. A pair of firemen gripped a limp hose, waiting for water. Two more firemen clutched axes, straining forward. But a familiar figure stood before them, arms spread, holding them back. Friedman had left his bridge game.

"The shot came from the house, Frank." In the white glare of a searchlight, Friedman quickly looked me up and down. "Christ, are you all right?"

"Yes." I was pacing slowly toward the far curb, making for the house. As I passed Friedman, I said, "Canelli's in the garage. He may be in shock. Send in a stretcher for him."

Suddenly the street was crowded with police cars and hurrying policemen. As I advanced on the house, a dozen officers fell in on either side of me, weapons drawn. I looked first at the service door. Still swinging, the splintered door hung in an empty doorway. The shot hadn't been Canelli's.

As I raised my eyes to scan the upstairs windows, seeking the gunman, I saw the blood-red front door opening. Wearing his black robe with its iridescent red Satan's head, Zeda materialized. In his right hand he clutched a large-caliber sporting rifle, pointed down toward the ground. Instantly, a searchlight picked him up. Again, Zeda was on stage.

In a low voice, speaking to the right and left, I said, "Don't shoot. Stay back. Cover me."

We met face to face on the sidewalk. Carrying the rifle easily at his side, Zeda looked like the Devil, off on a hunt through hell. Behind him, the leaping flames completed the macabre illusion.

With my revolver trained on his chest, I slowly extended my free hand. "Give me the gun, Zeda. Keep the muzzle down."

As he passed over the rifle, his satanic beard framed a derisive smile. His eyes mocked me as he said, "Muzzle down. Of course."

I passed the rifle to the man on the right and heard the bolt click open. Speaking very softly, I said, "You killed him. He's dead."

"I was helping, Lieutenant. Helping *you.* Leonard must've gone mad." He raised his shoulders in a languid, eloquent shrug.

I stepped close to him. My voice was hoarse with suppressed fury as I said, "You could have killed *her,* you degenerate son of a bitch. There was a woman in that car. *My* woman."

He faltered, falling back involuntarily. He moved his head from side to side, as if to seek help. Then his widening eyes fixed themselves on the muzzle of my revolver and I saw fear in his sorcerer's stare.

I placed my thumb on the revolver's hammer, deliberately drawing it through two deadly clicks. Again I closed the space between us. In the same hoarse voice I said, "You made Leonard kill King.

You planned it—set it up. You and the woman. *Didn't you?*" As I said it, I jammed the gun into his stomach, hard.

He began to shake his head with a sudden wall-eyed palsy.

"You had Leonard steal Clark's knife. Then you dressed him in blackface, and had him kill King—for money. The insurance. And now you killed Leonard, to shut him up. *Didn't you?*"

As I jabbed him again, I felt a hand on my shoulder. I heard Friedman's voice. I was stepping back, shaking my head—dazed. A stream of water shot by me, then another. Beneath the foaming arch of the second stream, I saw the porpoise shape of Canelli, lying on a stretcher as he smiled at me sheepishly. He held the big Magnum across his chest. As Friedman's grip tightened on my shoulder, I stepped back from Zeda, and lowered my gun, eased off the hammer, and slipped the gun into its holster.

Friedman ordered Zeda searched, cuffed, and taken away. Then, standing before me and speaking very deliberately, Friedman said, "As senior homicide lieutenant, Lieutenant, I am ordering you to turn around and walk over to your goddamn car. You are to get inside. You are then to take Ann home. You are to take care of yourself. You are also to take care of Ann. You might also like to change your clothes. Clear?"

I could only shake my head, allowing my eyes to close. I felt my body sagging helplessly. My knees were trembling.

"You look like hell," Friedman was saying, "and you smell worse than that. You're a mess. I don't want to see you until Monday. Tomorrow, maybe, I'll tell you how it all turns out. But I'll call you. Don't call me. Clear?"

I turned wordlessly away, walking toward my car.

Twenty-three

I said goodbye, rolled on my stomach, and replaced the bedside phone in its cradle. From the kitchen came the smell of frying bacon. I threw back the covers, got out of bed, and took my robe from a chair. Ann's clothing was draped neatly on a companion chair.

"I'm putting the eggs on, Frank," Ann called. "How many do you want?"

"Three."

I found my slippers, sketchily combed my hair, and shuffled into the kitchen. I felt curiously disembodied, as if I were recovering from an illness. I knew that feeling of disconnected reality; I recognized it as my body's reaction to tension and fear. And I realized that each year my body needed a longer time in which to restore itself. And my spirit, too. Especially my spirit. We'd come to my apartment last night, both of us exhausted, not speaking. I'd been obsessed with a shower—a long, hot shower. I'd stripped down, put my scorched, reeking clothes into a plastic refuse bag, and tied it tight. While I'd showered, Ann had taken the plastic bag into the garage, depositing it beside the garbage pails. Emerging from the shower, I'd found her in the bathrobe she kept in my closet. We'd gone immediately to bed, walking hand in hand into the bedroom—gravely, silently.

"Who was on the phone?" She gestured me to a seat at the table.

"Pete."

Her lips curved in a small, private smile. "Sometimes the two of you remind me of little boys playing cops and robbers, or cowboys and Indians, or something."

I snorted, sampling the coffee.

"You *do*," she insisted, sitting across the table and reaching for her napkin. "*Really*. You have all kinds of little games going, the two of you. And you don't even *realize* it."

"Games like let's fry Frank in burning oil, you mean."

Her gamin's smile persisted, even though her eyes momentarily darkened, shadowed by last night's terror. "That's exactly what I mean," she said. "The way you said that, I mean. So—so laconically. It's your role. And you play it beautifully, darling. You're the ever-so-serious hero in the white Stetson. And Pete is the—" She hesitated, frowning as she sipped her juice. "He's the dusty, lovable old saddle bum, I guess. And of course he gets all the good lines—and the laughs, too. And there are the villains, of course. The bad guys. And you all plan out how the game's going to go, just the way little boys do. You even squabble over who's going to get to be the hero this time, and who's not. Which confirms my opinion that—" She paused, eyes drifting away. I knew that mannerism. She was pursuing some new, wayward thought, hers alone.

"Which confirms my opinion," she repeated, "that a big reason for war is simply the fact that men are really just grown-up little boys playing with real bullets instead of toy caps. They—you—just can't leave guns alone. If little boys don't have guns, they use sticks and pretend."

As I salted and peppered my eggs, I thought about it. Before I could reply, she said in a low voice, "What I'm really doing, you know, is playing games myself—trying to be cheerful and gay, when actually"—she bit her lip—"actually, I—I can still see that— that leather mask, and that sword." She shuddered, then sharply shook her head, impatient with herself. For a moment we ate in silence, letting the shadow settle. Finally she asked, "What did Pete want?"

"Oh"—I sipped my coffee—"he just wanted to tell me how it all turned out, last night." I began to butter a slice of rye toast.

"Well?" she demanded.

Now it was my turn. "Let's change the subject. The less you talk about it, the sooner you get ov—"

"Listen, Lieutenant. I'll—I'll do something drastic to you the next time you try to seduce me."

I began nibbling the second piece of toast. "I don't really believe in seduction. At age forty-three, I've finally figured out that women are just smarter than men. Cooler. They—"

"Frank—" She sat with both hands flat on the table, glaring at me with dangerous eyes.

I sipped a little coffee, then said, "There really isn't much to tell. Pete—the boy homicide lieutenant—simply picked up Mrs. King and put her in one room and Zeda in another, and proceeded to tell each one that the other was blaming him for the two murders." I airily waved the toast. "It's really quite simple. Especially if you've done it for fifteen or twenty years."

"Did they confess?"

I shrugged. "Not really. And, anyhow, they'll both probably get off. But we have a pretty good idea what happened."

"*Well?*"

I smiled covertly. "Well, it seems that, in order to support Arnold Clark—the black guy—in a suitable style, Mrs. King started embezzling from her company. But a few months ago the company was almost sold. The deal didn't go through, but she got scared. Because if it *had* been sold, there'd've been an audit. And she felt that once the owners started thinking about selling, they'd stay with the idea. So she started to think about how nice it would be if her husband died—and she got the insurance. She apparently mentioned it to Zeda—although she of course says that Zeda mentioned it to her. Anyhow—" I drained the last of the coffee, and looked expectantly at the coffeepot on the stove.

"Keep talking." She picked up my cup.

"Anyhow, both Zeda and Marjorie King needed money, badly. Desperately. So Zeda agreed to 'do something' about Thomas King, in exchange for half the insurance money. He began following Thomas King, studying his habits. He also studied Mrs. King's habits. And then Zeda made a mistake. He decided to frame Arnold Clark for the King murder. He programmed Leonard—your friend the headsman—to steal Clark's knife, smear it with King's blood, and leave the knife at the scene of the crime. Which Leonard did, very effectively. He even dressed up in blackface."

"Excuse me, but do you mean that Zeda actually *controlled* Leonard? Like Svengali?"

"Back east, Leonard caused a girl's death. Zeda found out and held it over Leonard's head. For now, that's all we know. Anyhow, Leonard simply followed Thomas King around until he found the right opportunity, and he did the job. He carried a gun and his own knife, apparently. He knocked King out and stabbed him with the knife he carried. Then he carefully planted Clark's knife at the scene. Pete thinks Zeda drove the car and pulled the strings—and he's probably right. Then the next day Zeda called to tip us off—before someone disturbed the evidence."

"What about that hippie? The murdered boy?"

"Winship. He apparently stumbled on the scene, and got himself killed." I sugared my second cup of coffee.

"Did Zeda actually admit all this? Everything?"

"No. Most of what I've said is pure speculation. Most of it, in fact, comes from Mrs. King, who is still ticked off at Zeda for trying to frame Clark. Zeda, meanwhile, pretends to think that Leonard managed the murder, with Mrs. King's help. Which is easy to pretend, since Leonard's dead." I paused, then added, "Zeda's a hell of a rifle shot. I've got to give him that. It turns out he was a sniper in the Marines."

In a small, wan voice she said, "He might have saved my life."

I shrugged.

"It's incredible," she was saying. "Unbelievable. It's so—so *bizarre*."

"Yes."

She pressed the point. "To think that two people could plot a murder in cold blood. And then one of them gets a—a sorcerer's apprentice to do the killing. Not just one killing, but two—the same night. And then the sorcerer kills his apprentice." She shuddered. "All last night, I saw that sword slicing through the window of the car." Then, waywardly, her lips curved in a familiar pixy smile. "What are you going to tell your insurance company?"

My smile answered hers. "Cops have their own insurance set up. No ordinary insurance company will handle us."

"I can believe it," she answered. Then: "Why do you think they'll both get off?"

I shrugged. "This case is a potential gold mine of publicity. Even if they can't afford it, they'll have the very best lawyers. Wait and see."

We ate in silence for a moment. Then she asked, "How did you find out about Zeda?"

"We were suspicious of Mrs. King and had her followed. When she realized that Zeda had framed her boyfriend, she blew her cool and drove over to Zeda's house. That was Zeda's mistake—he didn't really think it would bother her that Clark had been framed. It probably never occurred to Zeda."

"The fatal flaw," she mused.

"What?"

"Zeda lacks the capacity for love. So he couldn't imagine her really loving Arnold Clark. It was a fatal flaw."

I snorted. "That depends on your definition of love. Personally, I'd call Mrs. King's feeling for Clark an obsession."

She stood up, rounded the table, and stood close beside me. I felt her fingers in my hair; I felt the warmth of her flank against my shoulder. She bent down to whisper in my ear, "What's wrong with being obsessed, Lieutenant?"

"Nothing, I guess. Not if you've got the weekend off." Still seated, I turned to her. As she arched her body, kissing the top of my head, I circled her hips with both arms, drawing her close.

About the Author

COLLIN WILCOX was born in Detroit and educated at Antioch College. He's been a San Franciscan since 1949, and lives in a Victorian house that he's "constantly remodeling with the help of two strong sons." In addition to writing a book a year, Mr. Wilcox designs and manufactures his own line of decorator lamps and wall plaques.